To Randy

Thanx
For your
help

& the Milkmen

Scenes In The Rearview Mirror

A Cabbies Journal

John "the Milkman" Wallin

Illustrations
by
Eric Downey

Front Cover
by
Sean Tuohy

AuthorHouse™
1663 Liberty Drive, Suite 200
Bloomington, IN 47403
www.authorhouse.com
Phone: 1-800-839-8640

This book is a work of fiction. People, places, events, and situations
are the product of the author's imagination. Any resemblance to actual
persons, living or dead, or historical events, is purely coincidental.

© 2009 John "the Milkman" Wallin. All rights reserved.

No part of this book may be reproduced, stored in
a retrieval system, or transmitted by any means
without the written permission of the author.

First published by AuthorHouse 4/29/2009

ISBN: 978-1-4389-5342-7 (sc)

Printed in the United States of America
Bloomington, Indiana

This book is printed on acid-free paper.

Dedication

To my Dad and my cousin Pastor Gary Wallin.

Acknowledgements

This project I have taken on has been the biggest and most rewarding I have ever completed. Without the encouragement and the support of hundreds of people, I wouldn't have completed it. I would like to thank the following people:

My awesome second cousin, Benjamin Wallin, who gave me great support and did some of my much needed research – especially the lyrics of the various songs.

One of my best friends, Sean Tuohy, who did the front cover for next to nothing. We had a lot of fun working on it together.

Thanks to my illustrator, Eric Downey for all the good times we had doing the illustrations when we would meet every two weeks at various hamburger joints.

My friend Ricky B. Bennett for his unconditional friendship and his support.

Todd Lilley of Carbon Copies for all the graphics on the front cover and helping me put the book together. Also for putting up with my nutty and punny sense of humor and for watching out for my special interests.

To my beautiful friend, Erin, for her patience and support.

And, of course, my friend, co-cabbie and dipspatcher, Dave Thompson who without his funny, witty personality, and wisdom, this book wouldn't be half as interesting.

And last, but not least, thanks to all my supporters and the following sponsors:

1. Bruce Tiger II
2. Brian Metcalf
3. Pastor Gary, Judy, Bethany, Rachael, Benjamin, and last but not least, Teerzah Wallin.
4. Paul Yaman Construction and Home Improvements
5. A&W, Cortland, N.Y.
6. Joe Kopp
7. Scott Gilmore
8. Area 51, Cortland, N.Y.
9. Luckys, Cortland, N.Y.
10. John Ryan
11. Carbon Copies
Main St., Cortland, N.Y.
12. Todd Lilley
13. Jennie (8675309) Jackson
14. Red Dragon Cortland, N.Y.

15. Tavern, Cortland, N.Y.
16. Palm Gardens, Cortland, N.Y.
17. Gable Inn, Cortland, N.Y.
18. Emily Feinstein – Hollywood Restaurant, Cortland, N.Y.
19. Check Mate Private Investigations
    Michael Bidwell CFI,LPI
    64 Main St. Cortland, N.Y.
    (607) 758-5441
20. Cortland Hardware, Cortland, N.Y.
21. Diane Nadge
22. Dr. Michael J. Shriro D.M.D.
    Star Dental Center
    Cortland, N.Y.
    (607) 758-3703
23. Cortland Hardware 37 North Main St. Cortland, N.Y.
24. Unfinished Furniture, Cortland, Ithaca N.Y.
25. Fiorent's Jewelry
26. K&H Motor Sports Little York, N.Y.
27. Eyewear Plus
    Walter J. Kasperek
    Optician/Owner
    Cortland, N.Y.
28. Cortland Clipper
    Al Atkins
    Cortland, N.Y.
29. Marks Pizza
    Owner Jared Carlton
    Cortland, N.Y.
30. Artcraft Home Improvements

Seeking Ithaca-Cortland
Area since 1981
Sidings, Windows, Decks
Roofs
Let us show you our work
(607) 7453242

31. Jays Taxi, Cortland, N.Y.
(607) 7535152

32. Maybury Bruok Stables
Visit us at www.mayburybrookstables.com
Trailriding, lessons and much much more!!

33. Dick Crosier

34. Katie Morris

35.Cortland Fitness
Market Place Mall, Cortland, N.Y.

36. Shear Obsession
A Full Service Salon
(607) 7565832
6 Homer Ave. Cortland, N.Y.

37. Tom Sunoco Repairs
Cortland, N.Y.

38. Frank Kennedy

39. Brook and Jay

40. Cortland Taxi, Cortland, N.Y.
Owner Ron Dolly
Call (607) 7565460

41. The Body Shop
Tattoo and Piercing by Gregg
Market Place Mall

Main St., Cortland, N.Y.

Alisa Beardslee

Tattoo Artist

42. Cahill, Knobel and Associates, LLC.
    12 South Main St., Homer, N.Y.
43. Elaine Contento
44. Mack Sams
45. Rae Marie and Dale Saddlemire
46. Rudolph
47. Tarik and J-Rod
48. Wanda Wawro
49. John Bush
50. Frank Hicks
51. Tim (Bus Driver)
52. Ruth Grunberg
53. Andy Goddard
54. Catholic Charities
55. Harold Johnston
56. Chad Phillips
57. Bob Marks
58. Ricky B. Bennett
59. Bill "the Grin" Grinell
60. Jeff "fat little buddy"
61. David Beal
62. D.J. Sonny King
    Visit our website
    www.djsonnyking.com
(607) 7569094
63. Dave Thompson
64. Jamie Alexander
65. Mitch Wooldridge
66. Ron and Patti Irish
67. Ralph Smith

68. Eric Downey
69. Eugene Murphy
70. Tom Vosburgh
71. Eric Bonawitz
72. Alfie Albro
73. Family Video
74. Mike Dexter
75. Brittany Pavlick
76. Russ Teeter

Contents

I	Forward	xvii
II	You Can't Make This Stuff Up	1
III	Police Log	26
IV	Joy Rides	68
V	Holiday Scenes	108
VI	Taxi Jams	159
VII	Singing Cabbie	211
VIII	This is Car 15…I'm Steppin' Out Momentarily	236
IX	King Harley's Roundtable	285

Foreward

Of all the roads I've been down, the one most traveled was when I drove a taxi-cab from 1997 to 2002. After a lengthy career of many careers—from being a radio personality to a telemarketer/salesman to a pizza delivery person—I chose the career of driving a taxi-cab from the encouragement of my friend and co-host, Dave Thompson. I no longer wanted to put all the repairs and mileage on my personal vehicle and thought that delivering people would be more lucrative than delivering pizzas. As it turned out, the money was twice as good.

I delivered pizza from 1992 to 1997, and every night after my shift ended at eleven o'clock, I would bring a pizza to Dave, wherever he was sitting in his cab. It was before all the cabbies started to take all the college students and townsfolk back home from all the college and city bars. I would sell the pizza I got for free to all the other drivers for

xvii

three dollars, but knowing I couldn't get away with that with Dave, I would give him the pizza for free.

One night when I told him that I no longer wanted to put the wear and tear on my car, he suggested I apply for my taxi license and join forces with the cab company he was working for. When I was approved for my license, I was hired, and my friend of five years became my co-cabbie and dipspatcher. We called whoever was dispatching "dipspatcher."

At first my new career was boring and mundane, but then I decided to spice things up a bit and reinvent my broadcasting career and—to a degree—singing skills. I would intro songs that came on my stereo to the customers that would request that of me. They had found out that I was a radio personality from 1985 to 1992 at 90.5 WSUC-FM, Cortland State University. I sang love songs off the top of my head to all the beautiful college girls I drove from place to place. One romantic evening when I picked up four sorority sisters from Alpha Phi, I started to sing a love song to the girl sitting in the front seat of my cab while her three sisters, sitting in the back, were giggling. I was nicknamed "the singing cabbie"; thus, the chapter 'The Singing Cabbie' was born.

The things that I spiced up and made exciting were under my control, but the crazy and dramatic things that happened, I wasn't in control of, so I had the whole

xviii

package. It turned out for the best because I got a book out of it.

My nickname "the Milkman," if you were wondering, was given to me by a "Dude" by the name of Mick Foley when I DJed the midday show after his show at WSUC-FM. I bought a half pint of milk to go with my lunch to my show every Wednesday, and as subtle and insignificant as it was, Mick picked up on it and gave me my nickname. I already had developed my radio personality and broadcasting skills, and had thousands of listeners in Central New York, and he just added the icing on the cake. Every time I came up to the station to do my show, he would drop what he was doing, take the needle off the record, and declare, "the Milkman has entered the building!" He was very selfless in that manner which aided to the growth of his own popularity. He went on to brilliantly promote his wrestling career and is currently an author of children's books, as hard to believe as that may be to those who know of him.

I hope you enjoy reading the following anecdotes as much as I have writing them. And though I have read them dozens of times, they still are funny and exciting to me.

You Can't Make This Stuff Up

…And here's the 90.5 WSUC-FM weather forecast. Overnight expect rain to turn into snow by morning. Lows in the teens. Tomorrow expect the snow to change to rain by noontime. You may see the sun peek through the clouds for the usual five seconds. Highs in the sixties. Tomorrow night strong winds with gusts up to seventy-five miles an hour. There will be a tornado watch until midnight. Expect overnight lows to dip into the single digits.

"Hey John, talking to yourself again?" A voice of one of my regular customers and friend said as I was waiting for the slowest light in Cortland to turn green. I was stopped at the corner of Main and Tompkins Streets where Ricky B. emerged from one of the college bars.

"No, I was just giving a sarcastic weather report on the crazy and *unusual* weather in Central New York."

John "the Milkman" Wallin

"That's cool." Ricky B. replied. "Would you mind if I cruised around with you for a while? I need to get the cobwebs out of my head."

"Sure, hop in," I replied, "and hang on to your hat."

Over the next couple of hours, Ricky saw some of the out-of-the-ordinary occurrences that I saw every night. When I dropped him off to his final destiny, he stated, "You can't make this stuff up."

Here are some of the more unusual and crazy incidents that happened to me over the five years that I drove a taxi-cab.

Date: July 4, 1997
Time: 6:03 pm
Holiday/Event: Independence Day
Occurrence: Hot Foot

One day I invited my friend Andy to ride around with me in my taxi-cab for a couple of hours so he could check out all of the beautiful sights (if you know what I mean). He thought that was a pretty good idea since he was coming to Cortland to go barhopping anyway. I told him to meet me at Smudgies Pizza at six o'clock. This would give him a couple of hours to ride around with me before the bars started to get busy.

Through the course of our two hour excursion, I noticed that he was really enjoying himself. He was flirting and socializing with the beautiful college girls that got into my cab. As we cruised down the main drag, where all the college bars were, a sharp dressed young man flagged me down and staggered into the back seat of my cab.

"Where are you going?" I asked.

"I'm going home to the Sherbrook Apartments. I've had way too much to drink," he managed to tell me. "Either of you guys have a light? I'm dying for a cigarette."

3

Andy replied, "Sure! Here's a book of matches, knock yourself out."

A few minutes later, I looked into the rearview mirror and saw a cloud of smoke surrounding the sharp dressed gentleman.

"What the hell?" I shouted. "Andy put that damn thing out!"

So Andy poured his sixty-four ounce big chug soda on the dude to put out the fire. "Are you all right?" I asked the gentleman. Andy simply shook his head in amazement.

"Yeah," the gentleman mumbled. "Let me out here. I'll walk the rest of the way. I need to cool off."

"OK. Don't worry about the three dollars. The ride is on me."

The sharp dressed gentleman limped out of the cab, minus one half of a pant leg, some singed hair on his bare leg and a bruised ego.

Upon later inspection, I determined the sharp dressed man must have flicked his cigarette, and the amber landed in one of the cuffs of his pants. I could only guess that he was too intoxicated to notice.

Scenes In The Rearview Mirror

John "the Milkman" Wallin

Date: February 23, 1998
Time: 9:00 pm
Holiday/Event: ---
Occurrence: Stella's Head Trip

The wind was howling and the moon was full. The night sky was unusually dark, except around the moon where you could see the clouds rushing past.

I was taking a regular customer of mine, Jeromy Hitchcock, to one of his favorite watering holes, The Lake Cuomo Inn, which was located eight miles northwest of Cortland. I picked him up at Kmart where he was buying something for his girlfriend who he was meeting at the bar. She lived in the village of Lake Cuomo.

Jeromy had told me previously that Sir Alfred Hitchcock, the famous movie director, was his uncle. When he first told me I didn't believe him, but when he asked me "how many other Hitchcocks do you know?" I took him more seriously.

Twenty minutes later, I pulled up in front of the Lake Cuomo Inn.

"I'll see you later, Jeromy. Say hi to Sir Alfred."

"I don't think I'll be seeing him for a long time," Jeromy replied. I then headed back to Cortland.

Scenes In The Rearview Mirror

When I got back to the city, I was given a call to pick up a girl from Another Planet Avenue. No one else wanted to deal with her, so, being that I was the new kid on the block, I got stuck with the prize. I usually picked her up every Saturday night. As I drove her from bar to bar, she drove me crazy. On this particular evening, she almost drove me over the edge.

I pulled up in front of her house, where she was waiting for me and she hopped into the back seat of my cab.

"What's your name?" she politely asked. This was about the twentieth time she rode with me, and the twentieth time she asked.

"John," I replied. I then mumbled, "For the twentieth time. What's yours?"

"I can't tell you that. You might start stalking me!"

"Alrighty, then!" I mumbled. "Where would you like to go this evening?"

"Murphy's, but drop me off down the block from it, OK?" she asked in a weak, but demanding tone.

"Why is that?"

"I don't want anyone to see me in a taxi-cab."

"Why?"

"Because everyone will think that I am poor and that I don't own a car," she replied in a whiny tone that would drive even the pope insane.

"OK then," I mumbled.

7

John "the Milkman" Wallin

"Thanks, Mr. taxi-man!" She happily shouted as I pulled up three doors down from the bar. "How much is that?"

"Three dineros," I replied.

"Three dollars!" she cried as she was shocked at the price.

"Yeah, three dollars."

"Well the other cab drivers only charge me one dollar, but I'll give you two."

"No, you won't. I am not like the other drivers. You will give me three dollars."

"Well now that you're being snotty about it, I'm going to give you only one dollar," she angrily stated.

"OK, give me the dollar. That will pay for your trip to the police station. The other two you can give me when you get out of jail for theft of services."

"Well," she calmly replied. "Here's the whole three dollars."

Scenes In The Rearview Mirror

Date: **August 10, 1999**
Time: **8:12 pm**
Holiday/Event: ---
Occurrence: **Dog Days of Summer**

It was a hot and sticky evening in the middle of summer, and I wasn't in the mood to put up with any drunks, let alone a sweaty and smelly dog.

One of my co-workers, whom I nicknamed "Droopy Dog," gave me a call to pick up a guy and his dog at the veterinarian's office on Madison Street. I gave him the nickname Droopy Dog because he sounded just like the cartoon character.

When I arrived at the vet's office, I noticed the dude had his pit bull with him. The dog jumped into the front seat, through the opened window, and the dude climbed into the back. I asked myself 'I wonder who the dominant one in this relationship is?'

The dog looked a little like Petey from *The Little Rascals*. She was predominately white, with a thick black ring around her right eye. She had a large elongated spot on her back that was shaped like the continent of Africa. The dude had long, greasy, slicked-back hair, a five-day stubble and a black patch over his left eye. He smelled like he hadn't showered in two weeks. I was kind of glad the dog jumped in the front seat because he smelled much better.

"There will be no sniffing of crotches, no drooling on my plush seat covers and no drinking from my cup of soda!" I exclaimed, sounding like Tom Hanks from the movie *Turner and Hooch*. "This is not your cab!"

We made our way down Main Street, past all of my fellow cabbies who were sitting in a parking lot, window chatting and having a meeting of the minds. My good looking customer just sat there with her tongue hanging out.

"Hey John, who's your new flame?" radioed Billy ("Bulldog"), one of my fellow cab drivers.

"She's not really interested in me. However, if you want, I can hook *you* up with her. You can also have her brother in the back seat." I double-checked the dude in the rearview mirror, and it looked like he had drool coming from his mouth. As it turned out, it was saliva on the mirror from the dog shaking its jowls.

I dropped off the dog and her owner at the animal shelter where she was going to be put up for adoption. I thought to myself, 'Hmm, maybe I should adopt the dog myself. She's really cute...nah; she would just chew my apartment up in a matter of minutes.'

The guy in the back seat paid the fare, and he and the dog disappeared into the SPCA.

Scenes In The Rearview Mirror

John "the Milkman" Wallin

Date: **March 21, 1999**
Time: **8:01 pm**
Holiday/Event: **First day of spring**
Occurrence: **My Personal Window Washer**

The last weekend before finals week was to begin at Cortland State University and all the college students were getting their last minute partying in. I was given a call to pick up a regular customer of mine named Gregg from Benny's Restaurant. He had just finished eating breakfast and was going home to his west campus dorm. Gregg was a twenty-nine year old returning college student. I had the radio turned to a classic rock station.

Gregg, who knew about my days as a radio D.J. asked, "Hey, Milkman, do your radio intro to this Eagles song for me, will ya?"

I was happy to oblige. "It's 2:45 in the am; you're rockin' out with "the Milkman". This is the Eagles with "Life in the Fast Lane", going out to Gregg on 90.5 WSUC-FM. Crank it up Cortland!"

Gregg then asked me to make a stop at the local convenience store so he could pick up a pack of cigarettes. Five minutes later, we pulled into the parking lot of the Mobil.

Scenes In The Rearview Mirror

Now mind you, Gregg was pretty wasted so I expected anything to happen at that point. When he came back out of the store, he started walking towards the gas island and told me to "watch this." He grabbed the window washer squeegee, walked back to the building and started washing the windows of the convenient store. He then walked over to car that was parked alongside the building with a guy sitting in it and began washing *his* windows. I was laughing so hard I couldn't contain myself. The store clerk inside rolled her eyes and probably said to herself, 'What a wacko!!'

When Gregg finally finished washing all of the windows, he hopped into the front seat of my cab. There were two young lovers sitting in the back seat who hopped in a few minutes before. They were going back to the Holiday Inn where they were staying.

As we headed down Tompkins Street in the opposite direction that Gregg was headed, he shouted, "Where the hell are you going, Milkman?!"

"I'm dropping these two people off first. It's only a couple of blocks out of the way."

"Dude, I need to get home. I have to be up in two hours to go to work," he stammered.

"Well, Gregg, I really don't think you're going to make roll call in two hours."

"Just take me home, all right?!" he demanded.

13

John "the Milkman" Wallin

The kid in the back mumbled to his girlfriend, "What a jerk!"

"What did you call me, College Boy?!" Gregg shouted.

"Uh, a jerk?" the dude replied.

"Just shut your mouth and start necking with your woman there before I break your neck and you won't be able to neck anymore."

"Uh, OK, whatever you say," College Boy timidly replied.

"Take me home first, Milkman," Gregg demanded, "so these two lovebirds can have more time to neck."

"OK," I diplomatically replied.

After I brought Gregg home, I dropped the two lovebirds off at the Holiday Inn, and went back to cruising down the streets.

Scenes In The Rearview Mirror

Date: June 21, 2001
Time: 1:09 am
Holiday/Event: ---
Occurrence: Action, Camera, Roll 'im!

I've seen pretty funny things before, but this takes the cake.

"Go get Tom at the Armadillo, Dave radioed.

"I'm after it. Where is he going?"

"He's going to Sherry's bar on Homer Avenue."

"Thanks, Ol' Grey Mighty One."

A few minutes later when I pulled up in front of the Armadillo, I could see a friend of mine named Zach. He was standing near the entrance checking IDs. He had a black belt in karate, and he was the only bouncer because he could pretty much take on the whole bar.

"Hey, Zach," I shouted as I was beeping my horn.

"Yeah John, what's up?" he answered as he approached my cab.

"Is Tom in there?"

"I haven't seen him. The place is really packed and he may have slipped in while I wasn't looking. Let me go check for you."

"Thanks, Zach. I'll wait for ya."

John "the Milkman" Wallin

A few minutes later he came out shaking his head and signaled to me that he had to go back in to break up a fight.

"OK Zach, I'll catch ya later."

"Hey Dave, I can't find Tom. Do you have any calls waiting?"

"That's funny," Dave returned. "We've been picking him up on Saturday night around this time for the past five years. He's always on time. Oh well, just cruise the streets and see if you can find any stand calls."

"Okey Dokey, you old stogie," I obnoxiously replied.

"Don't start! I'm not in the mood for any of your shenanigans."

So I spent the next couple of hours cleaning the city streets of the lingering party-goers. Dave wasn't feeling too well and decided to go home. When there wasn't a soul to be seen, except for the street sweeper cleaning up after what looked like a ticker tape parade, I decided to park my cab and take a snooze. I had just started to doze off when the phone rang.

"Taxi, can I help you?"

"Yeah John, this is Tom. Can you pick me up?" His voice was breaking up, and it sounded like he just woke up.

"Sure Tom, where are you?"

16

Scenes In The Rearview Mirror

"I'm not sure, but it looks like I'm at the Riverside Shopping Center by P&C Grocery Mart."

"OK, Tom; Hang tight. I'll be up to grab you in five minutes." I thought to myself 'He doesn't know where he is?'

I cruised over to the Riverside Shopping Center and saw a guy sitting in his boxer shorts underneath the phone booth as I approached P&C. When I got really close, I noticed that it was Tom. His hair was all messed up, and his glasses were half way drooped to one side.

"Holy crap!" I shouted. "Hey Tom, are you all right?"

"Yeah, just get me home, OK?" He was extremely disoriented.

"What the hell happened to you?"

"I'm not sure, but I fell asleep under this phone booth, and when I woke up the only thing I owned was my boxer shorts. A bunch of dudes rolled me."

"You're kidding?!" I responded. I could feel a smirk coming to my face, but I had to control myself. It was actually one of the funniest things I had ever seen. "Did they get your wallet?"

"Yeah, the bums. If I ever get my hands on them," Tom threatened.

I was still trying to stop myself from busting out laughing. "Hop in. I'll drive you home."

John "the Milkman" Wallin

When I arrived at his house, I told him that the fare was three dollars. I figured I'd have a little fun with him.

"That will be three bucks, Tom."

"I can't pay you because I don't have any money," he replied.

"Don't worry. Just buy me a beer some night." I could see a smirk on Tom's face. "You realize, Tom, I'm not going to let you live this one down." We looked at each other and busted out laughing.

"Yeah, yeah, I know. I guess if the shoe was on the other foot, I would be laughing at you."

"You mean the boxer shorts, don't you?"

"Yeah, whatever."

So I made sure Tom got into his house all right, and took to the city streets to see if I could find any other would-be riders.

Scenes In The Rearview Mirror

Date: May 10, 2002
Time: 3:39 am
Holiday/Event: ---
Occurrence: The Burning Couch

Beer cans, chairs, rolls of toilet paper, an exit sign, a dart board, dishes...a wheelchair?! Oh yeah, that must be the same one I saw a college dude riding down West Court Street at about twenty-five mph a few days before. He and his buddies must have borrowed it from one of the local drug stores...an ironing board, books, magazines, a TV stand, a portable radio, an old pair of sneakers hanging over the telephone wires, an empty beer keg and a street sign that bared the name of Clayton Ave., lying across the sidewalk...don't ask.

"Boy, these college students are insane," I commented over the radio to Dave and Norm. I was driving down Clayton Avenue looking for anyone who might have needed a ride.

"Why is that?" Norm asked in his really deep sounding bass voice. Norm had the perfect voice to be a disc jockey.

"It looks like the students just decided to throw all of their belongings on to the road instead of taking them home for the summer. There are some clothes, chairs, a

John "the Milkman" Wallin

bunch of broken bottles...Whoops, speaking of bottles, some kid just threw one at my cab. This place is like a war zone!"

"You'd better get the hell out of there!" Dave radioed.

As I began to make my exit towards the bottom of the hill to Main Street, I could see a young college woman flagging me down. I put the pedal to the metal, and snagged my fare.

"Where are you going?" I asked the young woman as she hopped into the back seat of my cab.

"Any place but here," she replied. "I need to get away from my boyfriend."

"Yeah, I think we both better get the hell out of here. What's up with these crazy college kids, anyway?"

"Well, for one thing, they're pissed off that they weren't allowed to have their block party this year. For another, they're just raising hell because it's the last weekend before finals."

In previous years the college students had two block parties; one at the beginning of the fall semester, and again at the end of the spring semester. There was a lot of trouble at some of the previous parties, so the college decided to discontinue them.

"So where do you want to go?" I asked the young college woman.

20

Scenes In The Rearview Mirror

"Take me to my sorority house, Nu Sigma Chi, up on Prospect," she replied.

"This is car fifteen, Dave, I have a stand call and she's going up to Prospect."

"That's nice," Dave answered in his 'big deal I've done this so many times' tone of voice.

As I looked into the rearview mirror, I could see that the girl was crying and really upset.

"It looks like you've had a rough night." I commented, sympathetically.

"Yeah, I just broke up with my boyfriend," she replied. "He treats me like dirt, and I don't want anything to do with him anymore."

"I'm sorry to hear about your troubles. I wouldn't worry too much. A pretty girl like yourself can probably just about get any guy she wants."

"Thanks Mr. Cabbie," she responded as she wiped the tears from her eyes. "You're a sweetheart."

"Hey, would you like to ride around with me for a while?" I offered. "That might cheer you up. Maybe you'll get to see some of the unusual things that I see every night."

"Sure, why not." She sounded like she was feeling better already.

"I'd better tell my dispatcher that I'm clear." "We're not allowed to have anyone riding around with us. I'll

21

have to make like I just dropped you off." "Hey Dave, I'm clear. Do you have any calls waiting?"

"No, just drive around and see what you can find."

So I cruised down the usual circuit with the girl still in my cab. This time, instead of starting at Degroat Hall, which sits at the top of the college hill, and at the top of Clayton, I started down at Casey Tower, which sat at the bottom of the hill on the other side of the campus. I didn't want to go anywhere near Clayton.

"It looks like things are starting to calm down around here," I said as I passed Casey Tower, and up the hill towards Clark and Alger Halls.

"Yeah, it's getting kind of late," the girl said, resignedly. "I think I'm just going to go home. Is that all right?"

"Sure," I replied as I headed up past Fitzgerald Hall, towards Degroat Hall and Prospect Terrace where the girl lived.

Just then, two campus security police cars and a city police car came screaming up the college hill road passing us at about sixty mph. We could also hear all of the fire engine sirens that sounded like they were coming from the direction of Clayton Avenue.

"Still want to go home?" I asked my passenger, knowing what her answer would be.

Scenes In The Rearview Mirror

"Hell no! Let's go check out what all of the excitement is about." She had a renewed spirit and sounded like Daisy Duke from the *Dukes of Hazzard*.

We took the long way around, down West Court Street to Main Street, and then over to Clayton, which runs parallel to West Court.

When we arrived at the intersection of Clayton and Main, we could see a big overstuffed couch on fire, half way up the college street.

"This place looks like Los Angeles after the Rodney King verdict," I shouted.

"Yeah, my boyfriend, or I should say my ex-boyfriend, probably had a hand in it," the young woman speculated. "He was really drunk when I left him earlier."

"I can't believe they actually dragged a couch out of one of those houses and set it on fire," I said in a tone of amazement. "This is car fifteen Dave; come on down to Clayton and check this out."

"What's going on?" Norm radioed.

"The students set a couch on fire in the middle of the road." I returned.

"I believe it," Dave interjected. He was already at the office where he was doing his cash up.

"Well, I'm going to pack it in for the night and head home," Norm radioed.

John "the Milkman" Wallin

"Yeah, so am I," I returned. "I'm going to gas her and clean her up. See you guys tomorrow."

"I'm glad I got to ride around with you a bit," the young college girl said. "You must see a lot of weird stuff out here."

"You've got that right. I'll take you home now."

So I dropped the young woman at home, and gassed and cleaned my cab.

"Hey Dave, I'm all gassed up and I'm heading to the office."

"OK, John. "You're not going to believe this, but I just heard over the scanner that the cops are going from house to house on Clayton Avenue, telling all the students that if they don't clean up their front yards, sidewalk and their share of the street, they are going to be arrested."

"Sounds like they are really pissed," I replied. "Oh well, such is the crazy life in the college town of Cortland, New York."

Scenes In The Rearview Mirror

Police Log

During the five years I drove a taxi, there were many times that I was involved, one way or another, with the local police. The majority of the times were minor incidents, but there were several times that I found myself smack dab in the middle of a major one.

Imagine yourself sitting with a dangerous criminal in the front of your car, or being handcuffed in the back of a police car because the cops think that you're a criminal.

Here are some of the interesting situations I found myself in the middle of, involving the police.

Scenes In The Rearview Mirror

Date: **February 8, 1997**
Time: **7:40 pm**
Holiday/Event: ---
Occurrence: **"Butchwhacked"**

One evening I was cruising down Main Street waiting for business to pick up. I was surfing through the channels of my stereo when I came to a song called "Renegade" by the famous rock 'n' roll group, Styx.

"The gig is up

The news is out

They've finally found me

The Renegade,

who had it made,

retrieved for a bounty.

Nevermore to go astray

This will be the end today,

of the wanted man..."

It reminded me of the night before, when I ran into a sheriff friend of mine at a local convenience store. He told me to keep an eye out while driving my taxi-cab for some guy that was on the top of their most wanted list. He told me that the guy's name was Butch and only gave me a very brief description of him. I thought the chances

27

of me running into the dude were very slim, so I didn't think much of it until the next night.

"Hey John, go get the Armadillo," Dave radioed.

"Okey dokey, I'm after it," I returned. "Where is he going?"

"To Onion Street."

I arrived in front of the bar and honked my horn, hoping that the person who called would hear it. The music coming from inside was very loud.

The guy came out of nowhere and hopped into the front seat of my cab.

"Where are you going?" I asked.

"I'm making a quick stop at a friend's house on the corner of Onion & Parti Street. "You'll have to wait for me when we get there because I need to be back here in fifteen minutes." He pulled out a bottle of whiskey and started to drink from it.

"Hey, put that down! You're not supposed to have an opened container of alcohol in the car," I sternly stated.

"Don't worry, just drive. I need this to kill the pain."

"What's wrong with you?"

"I got into a fight with a bunch of bros last night at a bar in Syracuse. One of the guys had a knife and used it on me."

"Keep it down!" I demanded. "It will cost me three hundred dollars if the cops see it."

28

Scenes In The Rearview Mirror

It never dawned on me that this could be the wanted criminal that I had been warned about.

A few moments later, I pulled in front of his friend's house.

"Here we are. Try to make it quick; I'm really busy."

"Yeah, yeah, just make sure you wait for me."

I didn't know what he was up to, but I could just imagine. It probably had something to do with drugs. I waited ten minutes, and I was about to take off when he emerged from the house. We headed back to the Armadillo.

"How much do I owe you?" he asked when we arrived at the bar a few minutes later.

"Six dollars."

As he rummaged through his pockets, he could only come up with three dollars. "Will this cover it?"

"No, the fare is six dollars."

"I'll tell you what, pick me up here at nine o'clock and I'll have the rest for you."

"OK, just make sure you're here. I don't have time for games. It's starting to get busy out."

After forty-five minutes and a few more fares I told Dave that I was going to head over to the Armadillo and pick up the dude. I waited in front of the bar for five minutes and decided to take off since he didn't show.

John "the Milkman" Wallin

"Dave, this guy hasn't shown up yet," I radioed. "Do you have any calls waiting?"

"No John, just drive around and see if you can find any stand calls."

"Okey Dokey."

I headed down Main Street and as I approached the four corners, I saw the guy walking arm in arm with a couple of his lady friends. He was walking towards the Armadillo. I also noticed Billy ("Bulldog"), one of my fellow cabbies, sitting in his cab kiddy corner to where I had stopped for a red light.

"Hey Bulldog," I radioed.

"Yeah, John."

"See that clown walking down the street with those two women?"

"Yeah, that's that dude, Butch, that the police are looking for," Bulldog informed me.

"No kidding!? I was told last night by a sheriff friend of mine that I should keep an eye out for him. The sheriff didn't give me a good description, so I had no idea it was him. That bum owes me some cab fare!"

"I wouldn't mess with him," Bulldog warned me, "he's really dangerous."

I was thinking of calling the sheriff's department on my cell phone, but then, out of nowhere, five police cars came flying past me up Main Street, the wrong way. They

30

Scenes In The Rearview Mirror

were traveling at a high rate of speed. Two sheriffs, two city policemen and a trooper were heading in the same direction as Butch. I went around the block to see what was going on. When I got there, the police already had Butch sprawled over the hood of one of their cars, ready to handcuff him. I guess someone else tipped them off.

John "the Milkman" Wallin

Date: July 14, 1998
Time: 8:03 pm
Holiday/Event: ---
Occurrence: Stuffed and Cuffed
(A Double Hit)

I've been accused of a lot of things before, but being 6'5" isn't one of them. Maybe if you were to switch those two numbers around, that would be more like it.

It was a very hot and muggy night, and things just weren't going my way. I was cruising down the road in my taxi, when I got a call from my *dip*spatcher, Dave.

"Hey, John Boy."

"Yeah, Bromo, what's up?" One of Dave's nicknames was Bromo because of all the Bromo Seltzer he took when things got stressful.

"Go get the Tavern. There's a girl who wants to go to Homer."

"Okey Dokey, Ol' Great Gaseous One."

"And then meet me behind the VFW."

"Why is that?" I replied in a suspicious tone.

"Because I want to show you who the gaseous one is."

"That's OK, Dave. I'd rather not get anywhere near that smell, if that's all right with you."

Scenes In The Rearview Mirror

"I'll show you who smells! Just go get your call!"

A few minutes later I pulled up in front of the Tavern and beeped the horn for my customer. While I was waiting, a police officer pulled up alongside of me, facing in the same direction.

"Can I help you, officer?" I yelled out of my opened window.

"Yeah, you know you are not allowed to be double-parked anywhere in the city," the police officer informed me.

"I've been driving for over a year now, and I haven't been told otherwise."

"You are supposed to park in a parking spot, if there is one available, within twenty parking spots in either direction of the bar. Pathetic!"

"How is my customer supposed to see me if I'm parked twenty parking spots from the bar?" I impatiently inquired.

"That's not my problem," the officer callously exclaimed. "Pathetic!'"

"I pick up people all the time in front of these bars and none of the cops have ever bothered me before."

"Yeah, well it's the law and you've been getting away with it up until now…Pathetic."

"You keep on saying, 'pathetic'. What is that, the new word of the week that you've learned?"

33

John "the Milkman" Wallin

"If you don't move, I'm going to give you a ticket."

"Speaking of pathetic, I'm getting really tired of being harassed by some of you guys. I'm just trying to make a living out here, you know?"

The cop then took off like a bat out of hell. I couldn't tell if he had a call, or if he just gave up on me out of frustration. After a few seconds of reflection, I conveniently decided that he lost the argument. I then mumbled to myself, "Hmph, that's tellin' 'im!"

A moment later my customer came out of the bar and jumped into the back seat of my cab.

"Where are you going?" I inquired.

"To Cayuga Street in Homer."

"Okey Dokey. Hey Dave, I've got my customer, and we're going to Homer."

"All right, car fifteen."

As we reached the Homer town line, I could see a Homer cop parked in front of a pizza parlor. He had his radar gun pointed right at me. I looked down at my speedometer and I saw the gauge at thirty-eight mph, just as I passed the police car. The speed limit was thirty-five. Sure enough, when I passed him, the flashing lights came on and the police officer started after me. I immediately pulled over and the police car stopped behind me. At first, nobody came out of the car, so I waited a few

34

Scenes In The Rearview Mirror

moments. Finally, an officer emerged and walked over to my vehicle.

"Can I see your license and registration please?"

"I was wondering what took you so long." I said to the officer as I retrieved my documents from the glove compartment.

I handed my license and registration over to the officer, and he told me that he would be right back.

"I'm sorry about this," I turned to my customer as she rolled up her eyes.

"I can walk from here," she replied.

"No, you'd better stay put for now."

A few moments later, the officer stepped out of his vehicle and made his way back towards my car.

"Are you from New York City?" the officer asked me.

"Yeah, why do you need to know?" I impatiently replied.

"Have you ever been in trouble down there?"

"I haven't been back there in ten years."

"Well, there's a warrant out for your arrest. Please step out of your vehicle," the officer commanded.

"This is ridiculous!" I responded as I stepped out of my cab. As I looked in the rearview mirror, I could see the girl rolling her eyes up again as her patience was growing

35

John "the Milkman" Wallin

thin. As she started to open up the door, the officer kicked it in on her and told her to stay put.

"Turn around please," the officer ordered. Just as he cuffed me and started me towards his patrol car, another police car pulled behind his.

"This is B.S.!" I yelled out as the second officer emerged from his car.

"What's going on?" the second officer asked the first officer.

"This guy has an outstanding warrant out of New York City," the first officer replied.

I was trying to think if I had any speeding tickets that I never took care of when I was down there, but nothing came to mind.

"Please step in the back of the patrol car," the first officer directed.

I was starting to get extremely agitated at that point. "Hey, are you going to arrest the girl in the back of my cab as well?" I sarcastically inquired. "Who knows, maybe she drove the getaway car when I robbed that bank down in New York City."

"Don't be a wise guy," the second officer insisted.

The first officer hopped in the front of his patrol car after he stuffed me in the back seat.

"What's going on here?" I inquired.

Scenes In The Rearview Mirror

"Take a look at the screen on my computer," he directed.

"Yeah, so what about it?"

"Your name is similar to this guy's name, so we have to check to see if it's you or not."

"That dude's name is John Walker, and if my spelling is as good as it always has been, Wallin is way different than Walker!"

John Walker's motor vehicle and criminal record ended where my name and record began.

I looked closer at the description of the dude from New York City and stated, "John Walker is 6'5" and Afro-American. Now I'm about a foot shy of that, and the last time I checked myself in the mirror, I had white skin.

"Yeah, well we have to double check these things," the cop continued.

"Whatever!" I was starting to get really pissed. "This is bullcrap. I'm going to sue the Village of Homer before this is over! Mark my word!"

"Relax buddy," the second officer said while he was talking with the first officer through the window.

Just then a call came over the officer's radio from their dispatcher, stating that everything checked out negative.

"What does that mean?" I impatiently inquired.

"You're all set to go," the first officer replied. "*Headquarters* had to do a more thorough check on you,

37

John "the Milkman" Wallin

and clear everything. They call it a double hit when two names are ninety-nine percent the same."

So the first officer stepped out of his car, let me out of the back and took the handcuffs off me. He then walked me back to my cab.

"I can't believe you guys!" I exclaimed.

"Well at least we're not giving you a ticket for speeding," the first officer replied.

"Yeah, yeah, whatever. I'm still going to sue the pants off of you guys."

I hopped in my cab, apologized to my customer and drove her home free of charge. Later that night, I heard that my boss's brother gave the Homer police a hard time when they pulled him over a few nights before. They must have gotten me confused with him, being that we look somewhat alike.

Scenes In The Rearview Mirror

Date: July 30, 1998
Time: 7:31 pm
Holiday/Event: ---
Occurrence: The Man in the Straw Hat

"Another hot and hazy one has blanketed the crown city of Cortland," the voice of the announcer said as I was surfing through the channels of my stereo. "Overnight lows are going to plummet into the low seventies. Expect another humid day tomorrow, with the mercury reaching 98° once again."

It was another slow night in the middle of summer, and I would have given anything to trade cars with my *dip*spatcher, Dave. He had the only car in the fleet with air conditioning that worked.

After about an hour of just sitting and sweltering in my taxi-cab, I was finally given a call to pick up 62 Scammel Street. When I arrived, there was a rather tall and slender gentleman sitting on the front steps. He was wearing blue-jean overalls, hiking boots and a straw hat that glistened underneath the baking sun. Barely able to stand up, he painstakingly put one foot in front of the other, and slowly made his way towards my cab. At first I thought that he was just extremely intoxicated, but later learned that it was more than just that.

39

John "the Milkman" Wallin

"Where are you going?" I asked after he climbed into the back seat.

"I don't know; just drive," the man with the straw hat ordered.

As we made our way down Church Street, I asked him once again where he was going.

"Uh um-um," he confusingly replied.

"I'm not sure I understand you. Where do you want to go?" I didn't get a response, but I sensed the gentleman was trying his hardest to tell me. "Where did you say you were going?"

He lifted his finger and pointed in the general direction of the courthouse park.

"I need to know where you are going, so I can drop you off and pick up the next person who calls." I began to grow impatient.

After I asked him a few more times I started to realize that something was definitely wrong, but I just couldn't figure out what it was.

When I looked into the rearview mirror, I could see the lethargic look on his face as he looked straight ahead without batting an eyelash.

"Car fifteen, have you picked up your fare yet?" Dave radioed.

"Yeah Dave, but I'm having some problems with him."

Scenes In The Rearview Mirror

"What's the problem?"

"I've been trying to find out where he is going, but I can't get a response from him. I've asked him at least a dozen times, but to no avail. He looks like he's comatose."

"Just tell him he has to tell you where he is going, or he'll have to get out of your cab."

"I don't think he's going to be able to do anything. He looks like he is in outer space somewhere."

"He's probably on some kind of drug. You'll have to bring him to the police station."

"All right, I'm on my way."

"I'll call the police station on my cell phone to let them know that you're on your way," Dave assisted.

"Thanks, Dave."

As I arrived at the police station, two city police officers were standing in front, waiting for me.

"What seems to be the problem?" asked the first officer who was in charge.

"This guy in the back seat is not responding to anything," I replied. "I have asked him several times where he wants to go, and he either tries to say something, or he just doesn't respond at all."

"All right, we'll take care of it," the second officer replied. "Hey buddy, what's your name?"

41

John "the Milkman" Wallin

"Hey pal, we are here to help you. Do you have any identification on you?"

"Try to get his wallet out of his back pocket," the first officer told the second officer.

As the second officer tried to get the wallet out, the man with the straw hat mumbled and wiggled.

"Sit still!" the second officer demanded. "If you don't cooperate with us, we're going to have to arrest you!"

He finally got the wallet out of the gentleman's pocket and started addressing him by his first name.

"Jim, what seems to be the problem?!" the second officer asked.

With no reply the first officer stated, "We're going to have to call for an ambulance. It appears that this guy is under the influence of some kind of narcotic."

Five minutes later, the ambulance came and the two police officers and the ambulance attendant had to practically pry the gentleman out of the backseat. When he realized that he was about ready to be taken to the hospital, he froze and didn't want to leave his temporary, but secure environment.

Scenes In The Rearview Mirror

Date: July 30, 1998
Time: 10:06 pm
Holiday/Event: ---
Occurrence: The Man in the Straw Hat—Part II
(A Lesson Learned is a Penny Saved)

"Hey John, go pick your buddy up at the emergency room," Dave radioed, in a humble tone of voice. "He has requested you and wants to pay what he owes for the last fare."

"OK. Hey Dave, should I charge him for the half hour I spent trying to take him home?"

"I don't know; that's up to you."

Five minutes later I pulled up in front of the emergency room at the hospital where the gentleman with the straw hat was waiting.

"Hop in," I said with a fresh new attitude. "Where are you going?"

"I'm going to 62 Scammel Street," the man in the straw hat replied. "I'm sorry for the problem I caused you earlier. I took my medicine and started drinking right afterward. I'm not supposed to be mixing the two."

"That's OK, it happens to the best of us."

We engaged in light conversation on the way to his house, and when we pulled up, the gentleman in the straw

John "the Milkman" Wallin

hat offered me a ten dollar bill and told me to keep the change.

"Don't worry, it's on me. Just take care of yourself and stay out of trouble."

"Thanks John, I really appreciate it," the man in the straw hat returned.

"No problem."

When he stepped out of my cab and started towards his house, I couldn't help feeling sympathetic towards him. He wasn't a troublemaker like many of the other drunks that I drove from place to place.

"How did you make out?" Dave radioed.

"Oh, pretty good."

"How much did you charge him?"

"I told him it was on me."

"Atta boy," Dave commended.

Dave rarely handed out an "Atta boy," but when he did, you knew you did a good job.

Scenes In The Rearview Mirror

Date: **May 5, 1999**
Time: **3:42 am**
Holiday/Event: ---
Occurrence: **Momentarily Deputized**

It was a crazy time of year. Spring was in the air, and the rising temperatures brought everyone's spirits up.

The college students were at the height of their partying, and soon they'd be gearing down to begin studying for their finals. As a result of all the partying there were a lot of shenanigans going on.

I had three separate calls in my cab: a local resident that I picked up from Easy Street Bar who was going home, a factory worker who had just come off his shift, and was also going home, and a college student who was going back to Clark Hall after a night of heavy drinking.

The college student, who was sitting in the front seat, was asking me a lot of irrelevant questions and seemed very nervous. From time to time he had his hand on the door handle. The two customers, who didn't know one another, were engaged in small town chit-chat in the back seat. I dropped the two off at their destination and proceeded to drive the college student back to Clark Hall.

"So how was your evening?" I asked in a leery tone of voice, laced with apprehension.

45

John "the Milkman" Wallin

"Oh, umm pre-pretty good," he nervously replied.

"How long have you been partying?"

"Oh, since about 5:30 am last night. Right around happy hour."

Once again, he was nervously holding on to the door handle. I thought he was going to jump out for a second. I then pulled up in front of Clark Hall.

"Well here we are. That will be three dollars."

"Uh, um, have a nice life," he said as he exited the cab.

As I looked in the rearview mirror, I noticed that there was a Public Safety Officer (University Policeman) writing out a ticket for an illegally parked car. I then laid on the horn.

"Hey, get that guy!" I shouted as I was pointing towards the runner. "He just ripped me off!"

I wouldn't have made such a big deal about three dollars, but it was the fifth time I had been ripped off in a week, and I was getting tired of it. The officer dropped his ticket pad and started running after the student.

"This is car fifteen;" I radioed to Dave, "I just had a student take off on me, and there is a police officer chasing him as we speak."

"Where are you?"

"I'm right in front of Clark Hall. The kid took off and ran towards the hill behind the dorms. I'm just waiting to see if the cop is going to catch him."

46

Scenes In The Rearview Mirror

I proceeded to drive up and down the college road where all the dorms were to see if the student would emerge from between any of the buildings. I also, over the next five minutes, went up and down the highway which ran parallel behind the dorms. I thought maybe I could spot him somewhere.

After another few minutes had elapsed, Dave radioed, "Hey John, where are you?"

"I'm going down Broadway Street in back of the dorms."

"Go meet that officer in the front of Clark Hall. He just called me on his cell phone to tell me that he just caught the kid."

"Cool. I'll be there in a few seconds."

As I went back around and approached the dorms, I could see the officer standing there with the kid. I pulled along side of them. The officer looked like he was going to have a stroke as he was huffing and puffing like a freight train that had come to a halt.

"Good job!" I rewarded the officer. "I can't believe you caught him,"

"Uh (huff—huff—puff—puff)," the officer replied. He was so out of breath he couldn't get a word out, so I figured I'd try my hand at momentarily portraying a police officer.

47

John "the Milkman" Wallin

"So did you learn your lesson?" I asked the student. "You know I could have you arrested right now for theft of services."

"I'm sorry, I must have lost my head," the student humbly replied. "Here's five dollars. Three dollars for the ride and a two dollar tip for you."

"What do you think officer?"

"I, uh (humph—huff—puff)," he laboriously responded.

"Have you learned your lesson?" I asked the perpetrator.

"Yes, I'm really sorry. This will never happen again," the student answered with a new tone of respect.

"Well I don't know, do you think we should cuff him and stuff him officer?"

"Well…i-it…is… (huff) – urghh – (puff) u-up t-to ya-you," the officer stammered.

"Well, it's obvious that you have learned your lesson," I firmly told the student. "But if I ever catch you again I will arrest you. You can go now."

"Thanks, officer, I mean cabbie," the student replied as he walked away.

"Thanks," I said to the officer, "I appreciate it. I'll buy you a cup of coffee and a donut some time."

"(Urrf – ugg.) Thanks for your help," he answered as he finally caught his breath.

48

Scenes In The Rearview Mirror

Date: November 14, 2000
Time: 1:59 am
Holiday/Event: ---
Occurrence: Saturday Night Window
                   Chat With Sonya

It was another Saturday night and the bars just started to close. I was taking Sandy, a regular customer of mine, home to Homer from Balducci's. Balducci's was a college bar where Sandy worked, partied, and just about made his second home.

I started thinking to myself, 'I wonder if Sonya is going to be easy to find tonight?' Sonya was a police officer in Homer, New York who I usually ran into every Saturday night. When we met up, we did our usual window chatting/socializing through our car windows.

I then looked up at the full moon and mumbled, "Nah, she's probably busy arresting all the troublemakers lurking in the shadows of the moon."

"What was that?" Sandy asked.

"I was wondering if Sonya was around."

"Oh. Let me off here, John. I'll walk the rest of the way home." Sandy usually got off a couple of blocks

49

John "the Milkman" Wallin

away from his home to wander and ponder the rest of the way. "Here's the fare, and a dollar for you."

I slowly started my way back towards Cortland, and guess who I ran into? You've got it. Sonya! I was doing the usual forty-five mph in a thirty-mile an hour speed zone when I passed her at the Homer High School. She had her trusty radar gun on and caught me red handed. She flicked on her high beams like she usually did when she wanted to say hi to me, and I pulled into the parking lot alongside her patrol car.

"Hey Sonya, how the heck are ya?" I was really glad to see her.

"OK, I guess. Do you know you were doing ten miles over the speed limit?"

"No, I didn't realize it. We're so busy and everything, and I was heading back to Cortland to see how many more drunks I could pick up and save from getting a D.W.I."

"Yeah, all right," she suspiciously, but patiently replied.

"What has been going on with you tonight?" I asked.

"Same old stuff," Sonya replied. "We're looking for a bunch of kids going around smashing in car windows."

50

Scenes In The Rearview Mirror

"Oh yeah? I had one of my car windows smashed in a couple of months ago." It cost me over one hundred dollars to replace."

"Yeah, we've been looking for these kids for over three months now, and we're hot on their trail."

"They're probably the same punks that broke my window," I deduced. "I'd like to get my hands on them."

"Car twenty-two," Sonya's dispatcher radioed.

"Car twenty-two, I'm here," Sonya returned.

"Meet the Cortland City Police over by Route 81 in Cortland, down by the overpass," the dispatcher directed. "They are after a bunch of kids that might be involved in those car window smashings."

"I'm on my way. I'll see you next week, John."

"I hope you catch the bums. I'll see you later Sonya."

Sonya took off so fast, I thought she was going to become airborne. It was as though she had a personal stake in the whole thing. I know I did.

"I'm heading back to Cortland, Dave."

"Where have you been?"

"I was talking to Sonya. They're looking for a bunch of kids who have been smashing car windows in. Do you have any calls waiting?"

51

John "the Milkman" Wallin

"No, just get the scooper out and see if there is anyone who needs a ride."

"I think I'm going to head over to the Route 81 overpass where Sonya was called to help chase down those thugs."

"I think you need to stay away from there and let them take care of their own affairs."

"Yeah, well you know, I have a stake in this as well."

When I arrived, there were three city police cars and Sonya in her patrol car. I was coming down Route 11 and I could see a bunch of kids running up the south side of the hill, towards the highway. The police couldn't see the kids because they were either under the bridge, or on the north side of the hill.

"Dave, call 911 on your cell phone and tell them that the kids are running up the hill on the south side of the highway," I radioed.

"Okey Dokey."

A moment or so later, I could see a couple of police officers chasing the kids back down the hill. They must have had a patrol car up on the highway as well.

"Thanks, Dave. It looks like they are just about ready to collar those losers."

"Good job, John," Dave rewarded.

Scenes In The Rearview Mirror

"Thanks. I probably will never get reimbursed for my own car window, but if it was those kids who smashed it in, at least I had a hand in catching them."

John "the Milkman" Wallin

Scenes In The Rearview Mirror

Date: **March 18, 2001**
Time: **3:18 am**
Holiday/Event: **Saint Paddy's Day**
(the following morning)
Occurrence: **Subconsciously Aware**

Every cab driver had his or her share of wackos every night. Maybe one or two a night would be par for the course—and that was more than enough. Of course I always had my full share, and then some.

On this particular night, being that it was St. Paddy's Day, we had more than our full share of drunks and wackos.

After the bars had closed, things quieted down relatively quickly since the next day was a workday. After a hectic and stressful night, I was just about to be sent home myself.

"Hey John," Dave radioed.

"Yessum?"

"I think we've cleaned the city up for the most part. You might as well gas her up and head on home. Bulldog and I can finish the shift up."

"Okey Dokey," I happily agreed.

As I headed for the nearest gas station, the phone rang.

55

John "the Milkman" Wallin

"Taxi," Dave answered. He was dispatching from his car.

"Yeah, I need a cab," said a voice that was partially slurred. It sounded like the guy was really drunk.

"OK, where would you like one?" You could hear the intolerant tone in Dave's voice, as he was having a very stressful night. "There are a lot of houses in Cortland," he wise cracked. "Do you have any particular place in mind?"

"Yeah, hold on. Hey Willie, what's your address here?"

"Eight Charles Street," came the voice of his friend in the background.

"Eight Charles Street," the caller relayed.

"OK, Willie, we'll be right over to get you," Dave answered.

"No, that's my friend's name. My name is Chaz!"

"OK, Spaz," Dave came back with a chuckle in his voice.

"Chaz! Chaz!" Chaz reiterated.

"OK Taz, we'll be right over to get you," Dave repeated with another chuckle in his voice. He then hung the phone up.

At this point I couldn't stop myself from laughing.

"OK Dave, I'll see you tomorrow. Have fun," I quickly radioed, thinking that Dave might give me the call.

56

Scenes In The Rearview Mirror

"Hold on John, I have to empty a kidney and get a cup of coffee. You'll have to get good ol' Chaz yourself."

"I thought you wanted me to go home! You just don't want to deal with Spaz, or Chaz, or whatever his name is. Passing the buck again, eh?"

"No, but I'm going to have to pass a kidney stone here in a minute if I don't get to the bathroom. Let me know when you get your fare," Dave chuckled. "I'm steppin' out."

"Yeah, yeah, whatever." I knew that he was full of a lot more than kidney stones.

When I turned on to Charles, the first house on the even numbered side of the street was ten. I figured maybe Chaz's friend Willie was drunker than he was and didn't know his own address. After a few minutes of waiting, out came Chaz stumbling down the sidewalk.

"Hop in," I yelled through the opened passenger side window.

"Can I get in the front?" Chaz stammered.

"Sure, why not," I hesitantly replied. "Where are you going?"

"To Homer," Chaz vaguely replied.

"Homer?" I couldn't resist. "Homer's a big place. Is there a particular street and house you're going to?"

"Yeah, 44 Cayuga Street."

John "the Milkman" Wallin

"Hey Dave, if you are back in, I'm going to 44 Cayuga in Homer," I radioed.

"Yep, I'm back in John. I'll see you when you get back."

Half way to Homer, Chaz started to fall asleep. I could see his eyes getting heavier and heavier, and his head start to fall forward. Every time that it looked like he was just about out for the count, I would either put my stereo louder, or cough real loud to keep him awake.

"Yo, Dude! Don't fall asleep on me! We only have a few minutes until we get to Cayuga Street!"

"I'm just dozing. I know what's gong on," Chaz replied.

Another minute or so elapsed, and Chaz started leaning towards me, as he was out for the count. I put my elbow up so he wouldn't use me as a pillow.

"Dude! Wake up!" I yelled as I pushed him back into an upright position. "You are going to have to wake up!" I started to make my turn onto Cayuga street.

Once again, he fell against me and I pushed him back up.

"Yo, Dave, you still out there?"

"Yeah John, what's up?"

"This guy is fast asleep and I can't wake him up." I had just pulled up to the front of his house.

58

Scenes In The Rearview Mirror

"Shake him really hard," Dave directed. "He'll wake up."

"He's out cold," I radioed after vigorously shaking the dude. "He won't budge."

"Just throw him out on the sidewalk," Bulldog callously interjected.

"No, I'm not that way," I returned.

"Why not? I've done it a hundred times," Bulldog boasted.

"Hey, Dave. Call a Homer cop, will ya? I've gotta get this guy into his house."

"All right," Dave answered. "I'll call them on my cell phone. I'll also come up to see if I could help you."

A moment later, Sonya, my favorite policewoman, came to the scene.

"What's going on?" Sonya asked.

"This guy looks like he's out cold and I can't get him to wake up."

"Hey buddy, wake up." Sonya shook him as hard as she could, but to no avail.

"Let me try," Dave offered after showing up at the scene.

"What are you doing?" Sonya asked.

"I'm pulling his chest hairs," Dave replied. "If that doesn't work, nothing will."

John "the Milkman" Wallin

"I'm going to have to call an ambulance," Sonya decided a few moments later. "Who knows what kind of drugs this guy might have taken, and how much he's had to drink along with them. Or maybe he's just being stubborn."

"Stubborn?" I was puzzled.

"Yeah, subconsciously this guy might know what's going on, but he doesn't want to co-operate. Things might change when they put him on the stretcher."

A few minutes later the ambulance arrived and the ambulatory attendants went into their routine after consulting with Sonya for a few minutes.

"Hey Chaz, wake up buddy," the first ambulance attendant demanded. It looked like he had run into this situation many times before. "All right, let's get him on the stretcher," he continued." The attendant wasn't going to waste any time monkeying around.

"I'll get the stretcher," the second attendant offered.

When they got the stretcher ready, the first attendant commanded, "OK, Sonya, on the count of three – lift!" Chaz was a good two hundred and fifty pounds and it took the three of them to get him on the stretcher.

"Arghhh (cough, cough)," Chaz grumbled as he sat up.

"So, you decided to wake up?" Sonya asked. "Didn't want to go to the hospital, eh?"

60

Scenes In The Rearview Mirror

"What are you talking about?" Chaz replied. He then hopped off the stretcher and started to walk away.

"Hang on a second!" Sonya instructed. "First, you need to pay the cab driver for the fare, and second I want to talk to you."

"Here ya go, cabbie. Thanks for the ride."

"Thanks Sonya. Let's go, John," Dave directed. "Let's leave Sonya to her business.

"Thanks Sonya, we'll see you later," I yelled.

So Dave and I took off as did the ambulance. As for Chaz, one could only guess what kind of lecture he received from Sonya.

John "the Milkman" Wallin

Date: **June 24, 2002**
Time: **1:19 am**
Holiday/Event: ---
Occurrence: **Brooklyn Bob**

"Car fifteen; go get Brooklyn Bob at the Cortland Diner," Dave radioed.

"Who's Brooklyn Bob?"

"You never picked up Brooklyn Bob before?"

"No, I can't say that I have!"

"You'll find out. Just go pick him up."

"I'm after it, old grey mighty one," I busted.

"You'll see who's old when you get Brooklyn Bob in your cab," Dave returned.

Three minutes later, I pulled up in front of the diner, and out came a tall and slender old man who looked like he was very drunk. He must have been at least eighty years old.

"Hop in," I politely yelled through the open passenger side window.

"No problem," he returned as he climbed into my cab. Everything seemed normal up until that point. Then, "What's all of this crap?!" He took my newspaper and threw it all over the back seat. Then he took my sandwich,

62

Scenes In The Rearview Mirror

threw it out the window and started to reach for my coffee.

"You touch that coffee and I'll break your fingers!" I warned. "Now get the hell out of my cab!"

"I'm sorry," he returned. "I've had a real rough night."

"That doesn't give you the right to trash my cab. Now get out!"

"Come on. I'll be on my best behavior from here on in." He sounded like the type of person who enjoyed giving people a hard time.

"All right then, behave yourself."

For the next five minutes, on the way to Brooklyn Bob's house, all I heard was why he was acting like a jerk, and how rough his day was. After I turned the corner of his street, he started in on me again.

"So, you think you're hot stuff don't ya? You cab drivers are all alike. You're all a bunch of rude and nasty bums."

"Don't start in on me again," I retaliated.

"Why, what are you going to do, kick me out?" Brooklyn Bob thought he had me just because he was less than a block from his house.

"No, but I'll tell you what, I'll take you up to the state land, eight miles away, and drop you off in the middle of nowhere. Then you can walk home. How does that sound?!"

"Yeah, you wouldn't have the nerve!"

"Try me, just try me!" I was getting really agitated.

I pulled up in front of the old coot's house and told him to get out – after he paid me, of course.

"Have a nice night, you old fart."

"Yeah, you too, you nasty old cab driver."

"Hey Dave, I'm clear with Brooklyn Bob." My mood had changed from being annoyed to being relieved.

"So how did you make out?!" Dave returned.

"Well, let me put it this way; I had a better time when I had my wisdom teeth pulled. I'm going to step out for a cup of coffee."

And later…The bars had just closed at 2:00 am, and it was time to cruise the strip to see what kind of business I could drum up. Most of the time the dispatcher let me run the stand calls as opposed to the calls that came in by phone because I was good at sniffing would-be riders out. Dave had gone home, and left the dispatching to my friend and co-worker, Jay.

"Did you get anything yet?" Jay ("Flipper") radioed. I nicknamed Jay, 'Flipper' because when he laughed, he sounded like the dolphin from the famous T.V. series, "Flipper."

64

Scenes In The Rearview Mirror

"No, but I'm going to head down Tompkins Ave. to see if any of the students walking home need a ride."

Suddenly, as I looked into the rearview mirror, I could see a bunch of bright, swirling, red lights. "Oh great, what the hell do these cops want now?" I mumbled to myself. I then pulled over to the side and radioed, "Hey Jay, you're not going to believe this, but I'm being pulled over by Cortland's finest."

"What did you do now?" Jay cracked.

"Nothing. You don't have to do much to get pulled over in this town." The spotlight was shining in my eyes as one of the officers walked up to my cab. The other one remained in the patrol car.

"Do you know why we pulled you over?" the first officer asked.

"I haven't a clue," I impatiently returned.

"We just received a call by a gentleman you just took home. He told us that you seemed to be intoxicated."

"Oh, that must be Brooklyn Bob, that old fart. He's a real pain in the butt!"

"Would you mind stepping out of your vehicle?" the first officer firmly requested.

"I don't believe this!" I exclaimed as I stepped out of my cab. "I'm trying to do my job out here and this is the thanks I get. This is B.S.!"

John "the Milkman" Wallin

The second officer then stepped out of the patrol car and walked over to us.

"Should we give him a breathalyzer test?" the second officer asked the first officer.

"No, I think we should give him a field sobriety test first," the first officer suggested. "Now recite the last seven letters of the alphabet– backwards," the first officer demanded.

"z, y, x, w, v, u, t – B.S. – S.O.B." I couldn't resist being a smart aleck.

"I could tell that this one isn't going to cooperate," the second officer said to the first officer.

"Yeah, we'll have to give him the breathalyzer test," the first officer replied. "Now blow into this cabbie—and blow firmly."

I said under my breath, "Why don't you make like the wind and blow away." I'm kind of glad they didn't hear me.

So after I passed the preliminary breathalyzer test, the cops let me go and I radioed to Jay that I was back in service.

"What happened?" Jay asked.

"Brooklyn Bob called the police and told them that I was drinking. What a jerk."

As Jay opened up the mic, you could hear him trying not to laugh when he started to speak.

66

Scenes In The Rearview Mirror

"Just wait until I get that jerk in my cab again. I really am going to dump him off in the middle of nowhere," I concluded.

Joy Rides

I'll never forget the evening when I picked up fourteen college students from Degroat Hall going to one of the bars for happy hour -- they were all girls.

Nine times out of ten, when I picked up a group of college students, it was a mixture of guys and girls. They would literally sit on each other's laps, sometimes piled three high. At times, they would even lie down on top of one another like sardines so they could get as many in as possible. The different configurations were endless. Of course, the people stuck on the bottom would be screaming and gasping for air, and the ones on top would be laughing.

I used to tell the guys, who were usually eager to sit in the front, that I had a house rule (or should I say cab rule) that at least one girl had to sit up front with me. They would all laugh and the more aggressive girl of the bunch would hop in the front.

Scenes In The Rearview Mirror

With fourteen students at a dollar a piece, plus a six dollar tip, their fare amounted to twenty dollars. It took me five minutes, and if my math is correct I could safely say that it came to four dollars a minute. Not bad for five minute's work, eh? I just wish I could have taken them on a much longer ride. That would have been some joy ride.

Here are some of the longer joy rides that I experienced driving my cab.

John "the Milkman" Wallin

Date: February 11, 1998
Time: 8:00 pm
Holiday/Event: ----
Occurrence: Good Ol' Aunt Miriam

Aunt Miriam...what can I say? She was a great lady. She never told me how old she was, but my guess would be at least eighty years old. I hope I'm as full of vim and vigor when I reach her age.

"Car fifteen; go get Aunt Miriam at the VFW on Main Street," Dave radioed. "She's probably doing her weekly barhopping routine."

"I'm on my way," I replied.

"Be gentle with her, she's fragile. And keep both of your hands on the wheel!"

"No problem," I chuckled. "She's not my type anyway."

A few minutes later, I pulled up in front of the VFW, and there was Her Highness, Her Majesty -- good ol' Aunt Miriam. She barely stood five feet tall. She stood there with her walker and her pocketbook hanging from the basket, which was in front of the walker. She had a sharp tone to her voice when needed, but was very soft-spoken most of the time.

70

Scenes In The Rearview Mirror

"Hurry up!" she snapped, in her soft-spoken voice. "I don't have a minute to waste." I could hear a slight slur in her words. I helped her into the front seat, and put her walker in the trunk.

"Big night on the town, Aunt Miriam?" I queried.

"You betcha!" she grinned.

"Where are you going?"

"To the American Legion."

I nodded, and picked up the microphone to radio Dave. "I have Aunt Miriam, and we're going to the American Legion."

"Hey John, ask Aunt Miriam if she would mind if you picked up a couple of people on the way."

"Just as long as it's not too far out of the way," Aunt Miriam replied. "I have an agenda to follow."

"No problem, Dave," I said, relaying her reply over the radio. "She doesn't mind."

"Go get Basil's. They're going to Off-Track Betting (OTB). Also get 52 Prospect (Nu Sigma Chi). They're going to the Pasta Movie Theater," Dave ordered.

"Okey Dokey, boss," I replied, doing my impersonation of Iggy from the TV series *Taxi*.

I first picked up Basil's on Main Street, and then flew over the college hill to get Nu Sigma Chi, a local sorority house.

John "the Milkman" Wallin

"Wheeeee!" Aunt Miriam's hands went flying in the air as I flew over the hill.

"You sound like you're on your first roller coaster ride," I said.

"First -- last. What's the difference? I'm having a blast!" she cried.

"Oh, this is nothing, Aunt Miriam. You should see it when I'm driving all the college students around. I'm just trying to take it easy with you."

"Don't worry about me," she assured me. "I don't get to go out that often, and when I do, I like to let it all hang out!"

"Just take it easy," the gentleman sitting in the back seat from Basil's stated. "I'd like to get to the OTB in one piece."

We pulled up about three houses past 52 Prospect a few minutes later. I had overshot the three-story sorority house by three houses. "Hang on!" I called. I put the car in reverse, and we shot back to the house, and up the driveway, backwards. I gave the horn a good tap, waited a second, and then blasted it. I could see the gentleman sitting in the back seat rolling his eyes.

"Yeah! Right on!" Aunt Miriam yelled.

"Hop in the back!" I called to the two girls as they emerged from the house hurrying to my cab. "Aunt Miriam is in a hurry!"

Scenes In The Rearview Mirror

When they were all settled in, I asked, "Where are you guys going?"

"Well, we were going to the Pasta Movie Theater, but now we want to go to Jollywood Video," one of the girls replied. "We've decided to rent a movie instead."

"No problem," I said as I was plotting routes in my head. "I have to drop Aunt Miriam and the gentleman off first." Jollywood Video was way out of the way in the other direction.

"Don't worry about me, I'll take the ride," Aunt Miriam blasted. "I'm having a ball!"

"Yeah, well you can drop me off first at the OTB," the gentleman who sat in the back ordered. "I don't have time for these foolish games."

"Sheesh! What a grouch," Aunt Miriam mumbled under her breath.

A short time later, I pulled up in front of OTB. "OK, boss. Here ya go," I said to the man. "That will be three dineros. Win lots of money, will ya?"

"Win some for me too!" Aunt Miriam yelled as the gentleman exited the cab.

"OK, who's next? Aunt Miriam?" I asked, facetiously.

"Bite your tongue! Don't worry about me. Just do what you have to do," she instructed.

73

"Okey dokey." I turned to the microphone and radioed, "I'm clear at OTB Dave. The girls are going to Jollywood Video instead of the movie theater."

"What about Aunt Miriam? Did you drop her off?"

"No, she wants to go for the ride. She needs to clear the cobwebs out of her head."

Dave chuckled. "Now she's going to have to take another ride. When you're clear at Jollywood Video, pick up Pop's Food Markets going to Wheeler Ave."

"Okey dokey; you're the boss."

I dropped the people off who were going to Jollywood Video and headed for Pop's. As I pulled into the icy parking lot of the mega-grocery store, I called out, "Hang on, Aunt Miriam!"

"What? What are you doing? Wheee!" Aunt Miriam screamed as I went into a fish tail and then a three-sixty.

"I would have done a seven-twenty," I began, "but I didn't want to…" My voice trailed off as I realized Aunt Miriam was holding her chest. What's the matter, Aunt Miriam?!" I yelled.

"I need to take one of my nitro pills. "My doctor told me not to get too excited." She took out a pill box from the pocket of her coat, and quickly pulled a pill out with her frail and dainty fingers.

"I'm sorry," I apologized. "I didn't mean to overdo it."

Scenes In The Rearview Mirror

"No problem, she said, dismissing my remorse. "As soon as I pop one of these, I'll be as good as new."

"No, I'd better get you home. You've had enough excitement for one day."

"Oh, darn! I was just starting to have a great time!" Aunt Miriam complained as she swallowed the pill.

A moment later, I picked up the people at Pop's Food Market, dropped them off at their destination and pulled up at Aunt Miriam's apartment, which was a few blocks away. I retrieved her walker out of the trunk and helped her out of my cab. "Bye, Aunt Miriam," I called. "I'll see you next week."

"OK," she grinned. "Maybe we can go for another joy ride sometime."

I smiled back and replied, "Sure."

John "the Milkman" Wallin

Date: June 20, 1999
Time: 7:45 pm
Holiday/Event: Frog Pull Weekend
Occurrence: A Hop and a Leap
to the Frog Pull Inn

"Hey, John."

"Yeah, Dave?"

"Go pick up Pall Trinity. There's a girl there who's getting off her shift and wants to go to the Frog Pull Inn. She's in a hurry." The Frog Pull Inn is a hotel/bar in Preble, some five miles north of Cortland. Every year in the month of June, the owners have a wet tee-shirt contest and a frog-pull.

"No problem. I'm on my way."

When I pulled behind the factory several minutes later, there was a woman already waiting for me.

"Can you wait just a minute?" the woman asked. "I have to go make sure my car is locked up." She didn't want to take her car because she knew that she would be drinking.

"Sure, no problem," I replied.

Since the woman was in a hurry, I kept the engine running and in gear.

Scenes In The Rearview Mirror

"Where are you going?" I asked when she hopped into my cab.

"The Frog Pull Inn. If you make it there by eight, there will be an extra ten in it for you," the woman replied.

"No problem! Hang on!"

Now it was at best a fifteen minute ride to the Frog Pull Inn. It was ten minutes to eight, and I knew I had to do some tricky maneuvering to get her there on time.

"How long have you been driving a cab?" the woman asked as we flew through Cortland and Homer at fifty miles per hour.

"Just around two years now."

"That's cool." She looked out the front windshield and started to scowl. "Oh great! There are two cars ahead of us, and it looks like a couple of Sunday drivers going for a ride in the country."

"No problem! Hang on!" I shouted.

As I approached the forty-five mph sign, I saw that there weren't any cars in the on-coming lane. I put the pedal to the metal and proceeded to pass both cars.

"Boy! This car has balls!" the woman exclaimed. I could tell that the level of her adrenaline, like mine, had gone through the roof.

"Yeah, this car was a police car once, and it has great acceleration," I replied.

77

John "the Milkman" Wallin

"Well, you have six minutes to get me there on time, Mr. Andretti."

"I'll tell you what; if I don't make it there by the time that digital clock on the dashboard reaches 8:00 pm, then the ride is on me. Hang on!"

"I'm hanging on!" she shouted.

After passing the cars, I slowed down to about sixty-five mph and asked, "Why do you need to get there precisely at 8:00 pm?"

"I'm supposed to meet my boss there for cocktails. We're going to discuss a higher position that might be available."

"A higher position?"

"You know what I mean," she said with a wink. "You'd better get moving. It's now five minutes to eight. Oh great! There's an eighteen-wheeler up ahead. What are you going to do now, my knight in shining armor?"

"Watch this," I replied with a James Bond-ish tone in my voice. I decided to pass the truck as we approached the end of a passing zone. We barely made it back across the median before we hit on-coming traffic.

"Are you trying to give me a heart attack?" she shouted.

"You want me to get you there on time, don't you?"

78

Scenes In The Rearview Mirror

"Yeah, but this is ridiculous! You know, you're something else. You really are my knight in shining armor," she sighed, as the excitement level waned.

"Thanks. Well, here we are with one minute to spare."

"Here's the fare, and here's ten dollars for the bonus." She smiled and asked, "How long will you be working?"

"'Till five in the morning." I replied, wondering where this was going.

Her smile broadened. "Then I'll definitely be calling you for the return trip!"

I yelled as she made her way towards the bar, "Good luck with your meeting! You thought that was crazy? Wait 'till you see the fun that we're going to have on the trip back!"

As I exited the parking lot of the Frog Pull Inn, I looked into my rearview mirror and noticed my typist, Joanne Sykes, entering the bar with her arms raised in a victory fashion. She was soaking wet, and my only guess was that she had just won the wet tee-shirt contest.

John "the Milkman" Wallin

Date: **June 6, 2000**
Time: **7:39 pm**
Holiday/Event: ---
Occurrence: **Coldbrook Express**

Summer was just around the bend, and June was the month of the Frog-pull, motorcycle parades, hot air balloon fests, and just plain old summer fun and relaxation. The college students were on their summer vacation, business was slow, and it was time to let your hair down -- if you had any.

I had just started my twelve hour, 5:00 pm to 5:00 am, night shift. My partner in crime and usual *dip*spatcher, Dave Thompson and I, were given a call by Steve ("the Man") Dumond who was dispatching from the office. His car had broken down, so he decided to man the radio so Dave didn't have to answer the phone from his cab.

"Dave and John, go pick up Coldbrook Hunting Reserve," Steve radioed. "There's a bunch of guys who are on their hunting trip that need a ride. They want to go to Easy Street Bar and raise a little Cain for the evening."

Coldbrook Hunting reserve is some fifteen miles from Cortland. It is stocked with game for hunting purposes. There are different types of animals such as bison, wild boar, white tailed deer, elk and many others from all over

80

Scenes In The Rearview Mirror

North America. The grounds have over three hundred acres, and have living accommodations for hunters who come from all over.

"Boy," I whined, "I wish I could go out myself for the evening and let my hair down."

"Let your hair down?!" Dave chuckled over the radio. "You don't have enough hair to put a lock in your scrapbook!"

"Shut up!" I unwittingly replied as I did when I got bent out of shape.

"Just go get the call," Steve cut in, disrupting our squabbling. "You guys can discuss the matter later."

"Aye aye, El Capitan," I replied. Hey Dave, when was the last time you went out for a night on the town? 1940?" Dave was in his early eights – I mean fifties.

"Wise guy," Dave shot back. "You wish you had a tenth of the wisdom that I have."

"I think I'd rather be young and active, than old and wise and ready for the old folks' home."

"I'll tell you what, I can run circles around you in any category."

"All right, you guys," Steve interrupted. "Keep your comments to yourselves and just go get the call! You sound like a couple of kids!"

John "the Milkman" Wallin

"Dave, you take the lead," I radioed, ignoring Steve's directives. "I need someone who is old, wise and slow to pace me."

Coldbrook Road had some very rough parts to it. It was almost like being on a roller coaster. You had better have some good shocks on your vehicle, or at least drive down it very slow. Dave, of course, knew all this.

"I've seen your driving, John," he reminded me, "and you're right; you're going to need me to keep you from driving like a maniac."

Fifteen minutes later, we pulled into the driveway of the reserve, window to window, and began to chat. "Is this a time call, Dave?"

"Yep. We're about five minutes early," Dave replied. He found out about the time call the night before.

"Hey, Dave."

"Yeah, John?"

"What do they call a dog walking down the street with steel balls and no hind legs?"

"I don't know, John. What do they call a dog, walking down the street with steel balls and no hind legs?"

"Sparky," I chuckled.

"Please, Lord... make this five minutes go by super fast," Dave mumbled as he rolled his eyes.

"Do you have any better jokes to offer?" I asked.

82

Scenes In The Rearview Mirror

Just then, ten men came out of one of the cabins. "How did they all fit in there?" Dave wondered aloud. "From the looks of it, we probably should have brought another cab."

"Why's that?"

"These guys look like they average about two hundred and fifty pounds apiece."

"Ah, don't worry about it," I said, dismissing his comment. "These Chevy Caprices are built to withstand a lot of punishment."

"They should have weight capacity signs in these cabs like they do in elevators," Dave joked.

"Hey, Jamie! How the heck are ya?" I called to a man I recognized. Jamie was a friend of mine who managed the game reserve. He had been invited by the group of hunters to go partying with them.

"Pretty good, John. How about yourself?"

"Pretty good. Half of you can get in my car, and the other half in Dave's."

They all clamored into the two cabs, as per my instructions. Two of the guys voluntarily got into the front of my car, against my wishes, while the other three climbed in the back. To say the least, it was a very tight squeeze with two two-hundred and fifty pound dudes in the front. Dave made four guys from his party climb into the back, and the remaining one got into the front.

83

John "the Milkman" Wallin

This time I led the pack, and Dave followed. After a few minutes, we finally started to gain momentum. While Dave kept a steady speed, I increased my speed by ten miles per hour to make some time.

"John, you'd better slow down!" Dave cautioned over the radio. "You're going to bottom out!"

"Don't worry, old man. I can handle it." The guys were yelling and joking around in both cabs.

"Hey, John!" Jamie, who was sitting in the back, yelled. "Let's leave them in the dust!" They all started laughing.

Suddenly, we hit the wavy part of the road. It literally felt like we were on a roller coaster. You could hear the tires hitting the wheel-wells.

"Hey, let's ride around like this all night," one of the other men yelled. "This is a trip!"

"Yee-hah!" one of the guys in the front of my cab yelled as though he was riding a wild horse.

"Hey, Sparky!" Dave radioed from about ten car lengths behind. "You'd better slow down! I can see sparks coming from under your car!"

"Hey, Dave! You need to relax and have a little fun some time!"

We finally turned off Coldbrook Road, onto Route 281, and made our way back to Cortland where we dropped the ten men off at Easy Street Bar.

Scenes In The Rearview Mirror

Date: May 28, 2001
Time: 7:11 pm
Holiday/Event: ----
Occurrence: Out-Foxed

It was my turn, once again, to pick up the boss's uncle from Beer Barrels in Groton, eight miles west of Cortland. None of the drivers liked to pick the old coot up because he was obnoxious, cantankerous, cynical, annoying, and to put it simply, a big pain in the butt. He was at least seventy-five years old with a lot of money to burn, and in his declining years, not a care in the world.

Every time I picked him up, he always had something up his sleeve. I didn't mind the little games he played, like making me come into the bar to get him when he knew I was outside waiting, or making me wait for fifteen minutes while he slowly finished his drink, or even paying me with a hundred dollar bill when he knew I probably didn't have change. I got stiffed twice on that trick. But I just couldn't tolerate this one time, which turned out to be the last time I picked him up. It was the straw that broke the camel's back.

"Hey John-Boy," Dave radioed, "go pick up Uncle Stan at Beer Barrels."

85

John "the Milkman" Wallin

"That's OK, you can send someone else. I'm not in the mood for his shenanigans."

"You know the deal. We all take turns, and you're next."

"That's right," Little Indian stepped in. "I picked him up last time and you follow me." He obviously didn't want to pick him up either.

"You sound like a bunch of kids," I mumbled. "I'm after it."

Ten minutes later, I pulled up in front of Beer Barrels and went inside to fish the old buzzard out.

"Hey Stan!" I yelled above the bar room noise as I got closer to him.

"Oh yeah," Stan replied, acting like he forgot. "Just give me a few minutes to finish my beer." He thought that I was going to stand there and wait for him, like the last time when I waited for him for ten minutes.

"All right, no problem," I reciprocated. "I'm going to get a couple of slices of pizza next door. Just come on out when you're ready." I thought it was time to out-fox the old fox and beat him at his own game.

I went next door to get a couple of slices of pizza and when I came out, Uncle Stan was already sitting in my cab.

"That was fast!" I exclaimed. "Usually you make me wait ten or fifteen minutes."

86

Scenes In The Rearview Mirror

"Yeah, well I'm tired and I want to get home."

Soon after, we headed back to the highway. He noticed that I was trying to get a piece of pizza out of the carryout box with great difficulty.

"Here, let me help you." Stan offered while I got myself situated. He grabbed the steering wheel and just as I got the slice out of the box, he grabbed hold of the wheel and yanked to the right.

"Are you crazy?!" I yelled as we started going off the road at fifty miles an hour. I grabbed the wheel, and steered back onto the road, regaining control.

"You're a frickin' idiot!" I exclaimed. "Are you trying to kill the both of us?!" With no reply, Uncle Stan just sat there and laughed. Then something snapped. It was like a bunch of chemicals in my brain coming together to create a massive explosion. "Oh yeah, you want to play games, do ya?" I drove into a field that we were passing and I could see the grin disappear from Uncle Stan's face.

"Hey, sla-ow da-down." Uncle Stan's voice was as rough and bumpy as the field that we were driving through. "Ya-ya ou're i-in-sa-sane!"

"Yeah, well you haven't seen anything yet!" I shouted as I pulled a u-turn about a hundred yards in.

"Le-et m-me out, ri-ight na-now!"

"No way, old man. I'm going to take you for the ride of your life."

87

John "the Milkman" Wallin

After I got back to the highway, I made a left on the road that Uncle Stan lived on, about a half a mile further down. Uncle Stan was as white as a ghost.

"You'd better watch these curves!" Uncle Stan yelled. "This road is very dangerous!"

I didn't dare heed his warning at that point. I was having too much fun. I sped up to around sixty, and nearly went off the road at one of the curves.

We finally approached Uncle Stan's house, and I pulled into the driveway.

"That will be fifteen dollars, Uncle Stan. I hope you've enjoyed the ride."

Uncle Stan was speechless. He reached into his pocket and plucked a hundred dollar bill from his fat billfold as he stepped out of my cab. He didn't even ask me for the change. I wished him a nice evening, and away he went with a dazed look upon his face.

Scenes In The Rearview Mirror

Date: May 15, 2002
Time: 2:00 am
Holiday/Event: **Graduation weekend**
                              at Cortland State
Occurrence: **Renee's Joy Ride**

"Are you back in yet, car fifteen?" Dave, my *dip*spatcher asked.

"Yes, I'm in."

"Go get ninety-five Tompkins. There's a girl that has requested your service."

"Cool. It must be Renee."

Renee was a communications major at Cortland State University who disc-jockeyed at WSUC-FM, my old radio station. She was a five-foot brunette, and had the cutest dimples I have ever seen. And let me tell you, she was a living doll.

When I pulled in front of ninety-five Tompkins, there stood Renee with two of her friends. "Hey, Milkman!" she yelled as she and her friends clamored into the car. "How are you?"

"Pretty good; where are you going?"

"Well, we're not really sure. Can you take us to the gas station first? We want to buy some cigarettes, and then we'll decide."

89

John "the Milkman" Wallin

"No problem," I said as I pulled away. "For you == anything!"

"You're such a sweetheart, Milkman."

"So are you, Renee. I wish you were mine," I mumbled under my breath.

"What did you say?"

I raised my voice. "I said you make me feel fine."

"Oh. We'll be right back," Renee yelled after I pulled into the gas station.

A few minutes later, the three sweet looking ladies hopped back into my cab.

"So, where do you guys want to go?" I asked.

"Just drive around for a bit, and we'll decide," Renee replied.

"All right, you're the boss."

"Thanks, Milkman. We'll pay you for your time." A mischievous smile came to her face. "Hey, let's go for a joy ride like we did last time!"

"Sure! Let's do it! It's not that busy!"

"By the way, these are my two best friends, Carly and Bridgette."

"How are you ladies doing this evening?"

"We're doing really good, Milkman," Carly replied. "We've been partying since 4:00pm yesterday when we went to the Friday's Neighborhood Bar for happy hour.

Scenes In The Rearview Mirror

"Hey, Milkman," Renee directed, "go pull up to that group of college students flagging you down over there, and then take off."

"Sure!" That was one of Renee's favorite parts of the joy ride from the last time. I pulled up ahead, a short distance from the group of students. As they came close to the car, I gunned the engine and raced down the road away from their bewildered looks. Renee and her friends were in stitches.

I then went around the block and pulled up along side a woman stopped at a stop sign. I motioned her to roll down her window. "Hey, did you call a taxi?"

"No, I didn't."

"Well, if you ever need one, give us a call!"

"OK," the woman replied with a bewildered look on her face.

"You're a freakin' riot, Milkman!" Renee hysterically shouted. "I wish I wasn't graduating for another year. I'm having too much fun."

"So am I. You can't believe how much fun I'm having," I said under my breath.

"What's that Milkman?"

"Yeah, I wish you weren't done with school either."

"Take us to 11 Hill Street. There's an after-hours party going on."

91

"OK, Renee. What are you going to do when you leave Cortland?"

"I'm going over to England to live with my boyfriend and continue my college education."

"Oh, that's too bad. I thought we could get together," I commented below the din.

"What did you say, John?" She shouted to her friend, "Carly! Stop yelling, I can't hear the Milkman!"

"I hear they have really nice weather over there."

"Oh yeah, I can't wait."

"Well, here we are girls. Here is 11 Hill Street."

"How much, Milkman?"

"Don't worry, Renee. Let's just call this my graduation present to you."

"You're awesome," replied Renee as she gave me a hug and a kiss goodbye.

"So are you Renee. I'm going to miss you. See you guys later." I sadly watched her walk away, and most likely, out of my life forever.

"Hey, car fifteen, John, are you clear?" Dave radioed.

"Yep. I just dropped my sweetie Renee off and wished her a fare thee well."

"Oh, that's so sweet," Dave replied with a mushy tone of sarcasm in his voice.

Scenes In The Rearview Mirror

I ignored Dave's sarcastic tone. "Yeah, I just told her the trip was on me."

"Boy, you must really be sweet on her, not to charge her."

"Yeah well, you never know. She may come back to Cortland some day when she's a little more grown up, and maybe I can hook up with her."

"In your dreams, Milkman," Dave replied with a smart aleck tone. "I have another request for ya. Go get Liz at Clark Hall."

"Awesome," I replied as the memory of Renee faded into the distant past. I could only look forward to picking up another beautiful college girl who always requested me as well.

John "the Milkman" Wallin

Date: August 3, 2002
Time: 5:00 am
Holiday/Event: ---
Occurrence: Japanese Joy Ride

Our regular shift had ended, and we received a call from the Holiday Inn for eight people going to the Syracuse Airport. They wanted two cabs. Dave Churchill, otherwise known as D.C., and not to be confused with my *dips*patcher, Dave Thompson (D.T.) picked up the dispatch. The morning crew was just coming on, so D.C. and I took the call since it was a slow night, and we didn't make too much money.

We arrived at the Holiday Inn where eight stylishly groomed Japanese businessmen were waiting on the sidewalk with their luggage. "Which ones do you want to take, D.C.?" I radioed.

"It doesn't matter. Take your pick."

"All right, you take the four gentlemen to the left of the luggage, and I'll take the other four to the right."

So we loaded them up and took off up Route 81 to the Syracuse Airport. D.C. took the front position and I followed.

"What airline terminal are you guys going to?" I asked.

Scenes In The Rearview Mirror

They started speaking to me in their own language, but of course I couldn't understand a word they were saying.

"Hey D.C., do you speak Japanese?" I radioed.

"No, why?"

"Well, I'm trying to figure out what air terminal these people are going to."

"Hold on, let me see." There was a short pause. "They are going to American Airlines."   "How did you figure that?"

"They have it written down on their ticket. Use your head!"

"Oh, I never thought of that."

D.C. was a sixty-year-old ex-marine who stood only five-foot-five. He was still full of vim and vinegar, street smarts and wisdom, and didn't take anything from guys twice his size. Between D.C. and D.T. — especially D.T. — I gained a world of knowledge and wisdom. Even though I was some twenty years younger than both Daves, I didn't take any of their guff.

"Hey D.C., look on the ticket to see when their flight is."

"It's 8:00 pm. Why?"

"It's 7:30 pm now, and we just passed Tully." Tully was approximately a half an hour away from the Syracuse airport. "We'd better step on it!"

95

John "the Milkman" Wallin

"Good thinking," D.C. replied. "Atta boy! That's using your head!"

"Aw, shucks," I sarcastically replied. "What can I say?"

So away we went up Route 81, doing eighty miles an hour in a sixty-five mile an hour speed zone.

"Chung-ching-chine-chime-chin-chin-chin," came the anxiety filled speech of the four Japanese men in my cab. It sounded like they were getting the ride of their lives.

"Relax, I've been doing this for five years now, and I've only had seven accidents," I reacted with a chuckle. Although they didn't understand me, and I certainly didn't understand them, we communicated through body language, facial expressions, and intuitive sense.

D.C. and I pulled into the airport and arrived at the American terminal with ten minutes to spare. We got out of the cab and helped the eight Japanese businessmen with their luggage. One of the gentlemen from D.C.'s cab paid him the fare plus the tip. The fare came to eighty dollars == forty dollars per car == and then they added forty dollars for the tip.

"Here you go, John," D.C. offered. "Here's your share."

96

Scenes In The Rearview Mirror

I counted the stack he gave me. "There is only fifty dollars here, and if my math is still up to date, you owe me another ten dollars!"

"Yeah, well, I'm older and wiser than you, so I should get a larger percent."

"Yeah, you're also a shyster and a con, and you can't pull the wool over my eyes, so cough up the ten dollars!"

"You drive a hard bargain, John. I was just testing you. Here's the ten dollars."

"Thanks, D.C."

So, the Japanese people were happy because they made their plane, I was happy because I was paid in full, and D.C. was still his same old conniving self.

John "the Milkman" Wallin

Date: **August 14, 2002**
Time: **1:21 am**
Holiday/Event: ---
Occurrence: **Free Wheelin'**

By this time you probably have noticed that I was getting quite the reputation for being a free wheelin', crazy cab driver. I didn't mind because I always have lived life on the edge. It's more fun that way. I think it's a part of being the non-conforming and rebellious person that I have always been.

It was kind of fun trying to get a rise out of some of my customers since many of them always tried to get a rise out of me. We all knew each other, so it was all in fun.

Anyway, one of my fellow cabbies, Steve, and I, would always try to put one over on each other. I put an end to that when I took him for a joy ride one eventful evening.

He kind of kept a safe distance from me after that.

"Go get Steve "the man" at the Cortland Diner," Dave, my *dip*spatcher ordered.

"Okey dokey, I'm after it."

A few minutes later I pulled up in front of the diner and out came jumpin' jolly Steve Dumann.

98

Scenes In The Rearview Mirror

"Hop in, Steve," I yelled through the opened passenger side window.

"Oh no, it's you," Steve returned.

"What, what's the matter?"

"I don't mind having some grey hairs, but every time I get out of your cab I gain a hundred more of them."

"Look, do you want a ride or not?" I sternly asked.

"I guess I have no choice. I don't want to have to wait for another hour."

"Hang on to your hat," I yelled. I figured I'd play the part since I was such a crazy driver, according to Steve. "We're cruising at 30,000 feet. Please fasten your seat belt as we are about to experience some turbulence. Please be aware that your air masks descend from the light panel when we lose cabin pressure."

"Watch out for that orange barrel!" Steve screamed. "Oh Lord, please help me!"

"Don't worry; you're in good hands with your favorite cabbie."

"Yeah, whatever! Just slow down, will ya?!"

"I have to make time out here. It's real busy and I need the money."

"You are going to give me a heart attack!" Steve yelled.

John "the Milkman" Wallin

"You want me to get you home, don't ya?!" I figured I'd prolong Steve's journey, so I turned down the street before his street.

"Where the hell are you going?!" Steve yelled.

"Sorry man, I made the wrong turn."

"If you weren't in such a hurry to make that extra buck, you would have made the correct turn!"

"What was that?" I asked.

"Nothing."

"I'll tell you what, I'll turn down this street and cut back over to yours."

"Watch out!" Steve screamed.

I then decided to *cut corners* and went over some guy's driveway. I went across his lawn and out the driveway from the side of his house. I just missed the telephone pole that was on the corner.

"Watch out, you idiot!" Steve was starting to get really agitated. I hardly could keep myself from laughing.

"Sorry Steve," I yelled as I turned the next corner on the street where he lived. He then grabbed the mic off my dashboard and strenuously shrieked, "Dave, if you ever send this maniac to pick me up again, I'm going to shoot you!"

"Thanks, Steve, for the vote of confidence," I yelled as I dropped him off. "That will be five dollars." The fare was actually three dollars, but I wanted to have some more fun with him.

"Five dollars?!" Steve exclaimed.

"Yeah, five dollars; Three dollars for the fare, and two dollars for the entertainment."

"All I have is a ten dollar bill." Steve was in a real hurry. "Just keep the change. I'm outta' here."

"Thanks, you the man! I hope you had a pleasant trip," I yelled after his streaking form. "Do you want me to wait until you get in the door?" I asked bemusedly. My high beams shone towards his house.

"No! Please just leave," he exasperatedly demanded. "And turn those damn brights off!" I could see him rushing towards his house and up the stairs.

"Bye, Steve, I said out of the side of my mouth. "Hey Dave, I'm clear."

"What did you do to Steve?" Dave blasted.

"Nothing, just the usual joy ride."

"Yeah, I know your usual driving. Now, go get the Dark Horse! There's a bunch of kids that want to go to Route 215 towards Virgil!"

"Okey dokey, kemosabe. I'm after it."

A few minutes later I pulled up in front of the Dark Horse and six people stepped into my taxi. Two got in the front, four got in the back.

"Where are you guys going?"

John "the Milkman" Wallin

"Up route 215 towards Virgil," one of the dudes in the front replied.

"No problem." I then radioed, "I have my customers Dave, and we're headed to Route 215.

"All right John," Dave returned. "Just take it easy. We want to get them there in one piece." My customers were all talking and laughing. They didn't hear what Dave said.

"Hey cabbie, does this boat have any balls?" one of the guys sitting in the back obnoxiously asked. The cab was a 1989 Caprice station wagon which we called the "Party Wagon" because it once was a police car, and had a souped-up 8 cylinder engine for hot pursuit.

"Yup," I replied. "This was once a police car until a few years ago when they retired it." "Yeah, its pistons are probably all worn," the guy in the front continued.

I thought that it would be a good time to try out my crazy driving again. "Let's put the pedal to the metal and take this ride on heavy metal!" The cab went thirty to sixty in under four seconds.

"Slow down, cabbie! You're going to get us in an accident!" yelled the other dude in the back

"You shouldn't put my Sally down," I said, trying to impersonate a mad man.

102

Scenes In The Rearview Mirror

"This guy's nuts!" one of the girls sitting in the back screamed. "He gave his car a name! What is this, a page out of Stephen King's Christine?!"

"That's OK," I responded, "You can insult me all you want, but don't insult my Sally."

"Just get us home, cabbie!" the guy in the front demanded.

I turned onto Route 215, which was an uphill climb, and decided to gun my car again. "Now what do you think?" I asked as Sally ate up the steep hill at seventy mph.

"Yeah, all right; you win cabbie," the dude in the back seat conceded. "Please, just get us home."

"Hey cabbie," the dude in the front seat yelled. He had a newfound respect for Sally. "You just passed our house."

"Oh, sorry about that." I then slammed on my brakes and put my car in reverse.

"Slow down!" one of the girls sitting in the back seat yelled, "You're going to pass the house again!" They all started laughing as they realized that I was just messing with them.

It felt like we were on a ride at a carnival. After a couple of more times of passing their house, I finally stopped in front. "Here you go!" I yelled. "I hope you've

John "the Milkman" Wallin

enjoyed the ride." The dude in the front paid six dollars for the fare and a four dollar tip, to boot.

"Thanks, cabbie," one of the girls yelled as they made their way towards their house. "Next time we call a cab, we'll ask for you."

I thought to myself, 'Boy this cab driving is a lot of fun, and prosperous as well.'

I radioed, "I'm clear Dave."

"Bring it on back, John."

So I headed back down Route 215 that overlooked the sparkling city of Cortland.

Scenes In The Rearview Mirror

Date: **August 18, 2002**
Time: **5:06 pm**
Holiday/Event: **Happy Hour**
Occurrence: **Babe in the Golden Mustang**

One day I was rolling down the main strip in the city of Cortland, where all the popular bars were, hoping I would find a stand call. I was waiting at a light on Main Street, when this beautiful girl in a gold mustang pulled up alongside of me. I couldn't stop looking at her because she was so pretty. She looked over at me and revved her engine as *my* engine was revving out of control. She looked away, the light turned green and she drove off, leaving me in the dust.

As she was taking off, it dawned on me that she was an acquaintance and a fan of mine from my radio days, twelve years before. That would make her thirty-five at that point, and, if I may add, still pretty hot. I then took off after her, and stopped alongside of her at the next light.

"Hey Sue!" I yelled. "Don't you recognize me?"

"Oh yeah. How ya doing, Milkman?"

I excitedly answered, "I'm doing just great! How are you? Are you married yet?"

105

John "the Milkman" Wallin

"Yes, Milkman," she replied in her usual patient tone that I hadn't heard in years. I used to hit on her all the time.

"What have you been doing?"

"I work at the movie theatre in Ithaca. What have *you* been doing?"

"Well, as you can see I drive a cab. I'm thinking about getting back into radio though."

"That's great," she replied. "What else have you been doing?"

"I'm writing a book on all my taxi experiences."

"Cool!" What's the name of your book?"

"It's called **Scenes in the Rearview Mirror,** and I am going to put you in it."

"Great!" she replied with enthusiasm. "Drop by the movie theatre with a copy when it comes out. I'll let you in to see a movie for free."

"Sounds like a plan," I concluded.

"See ya, Milkman!"

"See ya, Sue."

She revved her engine as mine was still revving. She thought she was going to leave me in the dust, but she didn't realize that my taxi-cab was a Chevy Caprice station wagon, and was a police car at one time. We dragged with each other two miles out of the city, towards Virgil.

106

Scenes In The Rearview Mirror

We were neck in neck until she turned off one of the roads towards Dryden.

I mumbled to myself, "Well, I almost beat her"

Holiday Scenes

Like the gravitational pull of a full moon, a holiday can affect a person's mood and emotions.

When people are rushing around to get their last minute shopping done, especially around Christmas, they can get real stressed out. When it's finally time to let their hair down and go out and party, the effects of alcohol will only heighten their stressfulness.

The taxi-cab driver enters the scene when the partygoers enter the cab.

Here, I present to you some of the more interesting anecdotes involving the holidays.

Scenes In The Rearview Mirror

Date: December 31, 1997
Time: 11:47 pm
Holiday/Event: New Year's Eve
Occurrence: The Streets of Juan Valdez

It was New Year's Eve and my boss, Mr. Ebeneezer Scrooge, made it mandatory that all the drivers had to work. I figured I would make the best of it and have a little fun myself.

"Car fifteen; go pick up the Hollywood Restaurant," Dave, my *dip*spatcher instructed. "There are three young ladies who need a ride."

"I'll do my best, but it's kind of heavy you know," I joked.

"Don't be a wise guy! Just go pick up the call."

"I'm after it--you old grouch," I mumbled under my breath.

Shortly after I arrived in front of the Hollywood, as I waited for the young ladies, my friend Mike came out of the restaurant to wish me a Happy New Year. Mike is an old friend of mine who plays the electric guitar extremely well. He jams with Dave Fienstein, the owner of the Hollywood Restaurant, who played with Ronnie James Dio back in the sixties. Dio eventually played with Rainbow in the seventies and then Black Sabbath in

109

the early eighties. He started his solo career in the mid-eighties, and has been internationally successful with it ever since.

"I'll catch you around sometime," I yelled, as Mike went back into the restaurant. "Happy New Year!" Three young ladies came out and hopped into the back seat of my cab moments later.

"Where are you lovely ladies going?" I inquired.

"We're going to the Sneak Inn Motel in Pokeville," one of them replied, "but we were wondering if we could drive by Main Street to watch the ball drop from the clock tower?"

"Sure why not. I would like to watch it myself." It was getting very close to midnight.

As we made our way down Groton Avenue, a woman came out one of the bars and started walking across the street. She staggered right up to my cab, and as I swerved to miss her, by a matter of inches, she turned back towards the sidewalk.

"Holy crap!" I yelled. "This woman is nuts!"

As she started walking back across the street, another taxi that was coming the other way came just as close to hitting her as I did.

One of the women exclaimed, "That woman's not going to live to see the New Year!"

"You've got that right," I replied.

Scenes In The Rearview Mirror

Shortly after we arrived on Main Street, we were able to go as far as Central Avenue where everything was blocked off with police barricades. We had to go around the block to get to where the clock tower stood. Just in the nick of time, we pulled into the convenience store's parking lot across the street from the tower and watched the ball's descent to midnight.

"...Five, four, three, two, one!" the master of ceremonies and disc- jockey, Sonny King, yelled over the sound system. Sonny King is a local D.J. personality at WXHC in Homer, about two miles north of Cortland. He was the program director at FM 9.20 WSUC, from 1980 to 1991, where I disc-jockeyed professionally for three years--from 1988 to 1991.

The fireworks started flying all over the place, and everyone in the packed street was cheering.

"Would you like a sip of my champagne?" one of the young women offered.

"Just a sip," I replied. "I have to stay sober to drive all of the drunks around." We all toasted to the New Year.

After the brilliant display of fireworks, everyone in the street made their way towards South Main Street where their cars were parked.

"Car fifteen;" Dave radioed, "are you clear yet?"

I thought to myself, 'I can't wait for this crowd of hundreds of people to disperse. It's going to take fifteen or twenty minutes to get out of here!'

"Car fifteen;" Dave repeated, "What are you doing?"

"I'm trying to figure out how to get through this crowd of wall to wall people."

"Where are you right now?"

"I'm in the parking lot on South Main, across the street from the clock tower, and everyone is now in front of me making their way towards their cars."

"Oh, that was smart!" Dave came back with a note of sarcasm in his voice. "What are you going to do now?"

"Don't worry; you know me. I'm pretty good at getting out of these jams."

"Yeah, jams that you shouldn't get into in the first place!"

"Yeah, well you know, all work and no play makes Jack a dull boy."

"Hey, we don't mind hanging out, cabbie!" one of the women shouted. "This is really exciting out here!"

"No, I'd better get out of here. I have to get you guys home. And then I have to clean up the city and make sure everyone gets home all right."

I then started, inch by inch at about two miles per hour, making my way through the crowd. I started

Scenes In The Rearview Mirror

slapping everyone high five and yelled out my window, "Happy Freakin' New Year!"

I could remember some guy yelling out, "Hey, it's Juan Valdez!" making reference to the famous Columbian coffee maker who was in the popular coffee commercial back in the seventies.

John "the Milkman" Wallin

Scenes In The Rearview Mirror

Date: February 14, 1998
Time: 3:00 am
Holiday/Event: Valentine's Day
Occurrence: Shooting Stars

It was the middle of spring and it was unusually chilly for that time of year. The green leaves on the trees were still not fully grown, and the flower blossoms weren't sure if it was spring or autumn.

I was cruising down the college hill to see if I could get any after-the-bar-rush stand calls. My *dip*spatcher, Dave, told me to get my girls at 25 Clayton Avenue in Cortland. They were going to the TC3 dorms located in Dryden. Dryden is a village between Cortland and Ithaca that has Tompkins Cortland Community College (TC3), one gas station and ten pizza places. Many college professors and college employees from TC3, Cornell University and Ithaca College live there. Many of the students from Cortland State who weren't doing too well academically attended TC3 to get their grades back up. When they accomplished that, they would be accepted back into Cortland State. Both schools were in the same school system--State University of New York (SUNY).

When I pulled up in front of 25 Clayton Avenue, I saw that it was my friend Nina and her two friends. Nina

115

John "the Milkman" Wallin

was a drama major at Cortland State, and from the looks and sounds of her she most likely was going to make it on Broadway. She was a beautiful young woman with a lot of personality and a beautiful singing voice.

"I have Nina, the The Pinta, and The Santa Maria," I radioed to Dave as the three girls hopped into my cab. I turned to the girls and asked, "Where are you girls going?"

"Pinta and Santa Maria are going to Hayes hall, and I'm going to the TC3 dorms," Nina giggled.

"How have you been, Nina?" I asked. "I haven't seen you in a few weeks."

"I've been doing really well. School is going very well and I just recently landed the supporting role in a play at Cortland State."

"That's great! Hey, Nina, sing a Broadway tune," I conducted as I pressed in the microphone button to my radio.

"Turn that thing off," she bashfully replied.

"Come on, Nina," her friends coaxed and encouraged her.

"Yeah, come on Nina. It's your chance to shine in the spotlight," I winked.

"All right," Nina replied exasperated, bowing under the pressure.

116

Scenes In The Rearview Mirror

"The sun'll come out tomorrow
Bet your bottom dollar that tomorrow
there'll be sun
Just thinkin' about tomorrow
wash away your troubles and your sorrows
'till there's none..." Nina belted out.

"Good job, Nina," I commended.

"Who was that?" came Dave's voice over the radio.

"That's Nina, my leading lady," I replied.

"What, does she lead you around on a chain?" Dave cracked.

"Very funny, Dave. I didn't know you had such a jealous nature. I'm clear at Hayes Hall and I'm bringing my sweetie over to her friends' dorm at TC3."

"OK. Just keep both hands on the wheel."

"Yeah, all right. See ya when I get back." I switched the radio off and added under my breath, "If I come back at all."

Nina and I took off into the celestial night and headed towards Dryden. I stole glances at Nina whenever I could, and finally commented, "You know Nina, if I were ten years younger, I would ask you out."

117

John "the Milkman" Wallin

"Well, you know John," Nina replied with a sensuous tone in her voice, "I like older men."

"Oh, yeah? How would you like to go out to dinner and take in a movie some evening?" I asked the way a teenager would with his knees knocking together.

"Sure." Nina smiled. "I'll give you my number and you can call me when it's convenient for you." She wrote the number on a napkin and handed it to me.

We pulled into the TC3 dormitory circle in front of the Cayuga Dormitory. "Good night, Nina. I'll call you soon," I said as she paid for the fare.

"Good night John," she whispered as she leaned towards me to give me a kiss.

The kiss seemed to last forever until I opened one of my eyes and saw a bunch of shooting stars out my window. "Wow, I never saw shooting stars before when I kissed someone."

"Those are real, silly," Nina laughed as she gazed at the spectacle. "Didn't you know there is a meteor shower this morning 'till 5:00 am?"

I shook my head. "You shouldn't have told me, Nina. Being that I am a romantic, I wouldn't have minded thinking that it was you that made me see a bunch of shooting stars."

"You hopeless romantic, you. I'll see you soon."

118

Scenes In The Rearview Mirror

"OK, Nina, take care of yourself."

I left Nina and took off back to Cortland under the romantically lit night.

John "the Milkman" Wallin

Scenes In The Rearview Mirror

Date: **April 12, 1998**
Time: **6:14 pm**
Holiday/Event: **Easter Eve**
Occurrence: **The Invisible Stuffed Easter Bunny**

It was Easter Eve and everyone was out and about doing their last minute shopping for Easter Sunday. I was given a call to pick up a day driver who had to run an errand. Of course it was totally unrelated to the Easter holiday.

"Hey, car fifteen," Billy ("Bulldog") radioed from his car. They called Billy, "Bulldog" because of his rugged frame and his tough personality.

"Yeah, waas up?"

"Go get Jake at his house. He is going up to Syracuse."

"Why is he going to Syracuse?"

"I don't know. He didn't say."

"I'm after it."

A few minutes later, I pulled in front of Jake's house and leaned on the horn.

121

John "the Milkman" Wallin

"Hold your horses!" Jake yelled out his second story window.

"Hurry up!" I yelled back. "I don't have all day." I couldn't resist giving him a hard time since he always picked on me.

Ten minutes later, Jake came running out and hopped into my cab. "Why do you always have to beep that horn so loud?!" he shrieked with his whiny voice. We'd always beeped the horn for him when he didn't come out right away. After a while, we beeped the horn no matter what, just to annoy him.

"It's a force of habit," I shot back. "If you were ready on time every morning, we wouldn't have to beep the horn!" This was my way of bringing the subject up.

"Yeah, well you'd better stop beeping your horn at 5:00 in the morning. My girlfriend is getting pissed off. And besides, you don't need to beep the horn a hundred times!"

"What are you talking about? I only beep the horn once or twice. You're hearing all the other drivers beeping their horns every time they pass your house; I'm not the only one your tardiness inconveniences."

122

Scenes In The Rearview Mirror

"You guys are a bunch of maniacs, you know that?"

"Yeah, well we don't relish being out here after our shift ends just because you can't get yourself out of bed. Maybe you would be ready if you weren't out partying 'till 1:00 in the morning."

"Yeah, yeah, whatever."

"Where are you going?" I asked, after our usual five minutes of squabbling came to an end.

"I'm going to Syracuse to purchase something important." Jake thought that he was keeping me in the dark.

"More like something potent and illegal as well," I mumbled.

"What was that?" Jake snapped back.

"Nothing. This is car fifteen, Bulldog; I have Jake and we are on our way to Syracuse."

"Why are you going to Syracuse?" Bulldog asked, with a suspicious tone.

Several seconds of silence elapsed before I could think of anything to say. "He wants to buy his nephew a four foot wide by ten foot long stuffed bunny rabbit

John "the Milkman" Wallin

that he saw when he was up there a week ago." I had to say something to cover for Jake.

"Good cover-up," Jake commended.

When we arrived at his destination thirty-five miles and a half hour later, Jake took care of his personal business and we headed back to Cortland.

"Did you get your stuff, Jake?" I asked.

"Yep. Do you want to smoke some?" Jake inquired.

"No, I don't do that stuff. And you shouldn't either. That's why you're always late for work in the morning because you're partying all night long!"

"Don't start that again!"

A half hour later I was back in Cortland and I radioed to Bulldog, "This is car fifteen; Jake and I are back in town."

"Did you get the stuffed bunny rabbit?" Bulldog asked, with the enthusiasm of an eight year old.

"Yes we did, Bulldog," I condescendingly replied. "The damn thing is so big, its head and ears are sticking out of the back window of my station wagon. We had to put the back seat down to get the whole thing in."

124

Scenes In The Rearview Mirror

"Well, where are you? Can I see it?"

"No, I'm dropping Jake and the rabbit off as we speak."

"Oh," Bulldog responded with a tone of disappointment, as Jake and I laughed.

John "the Milkman" Wallin

Scenes In The Rearview Mirror

Date: June 6, 1998
Time: 6:03 pm
Holiday/Event: Cortland County Dairy Days
Occurrence: The Dairy Prince

Every year in June, Cortland County has a dairy holiday to celebrate one of the county's richest industries. Among the highlighted events are the dairy parade and the crowning of the Dairy Princess. Business had come to a halt, since everyone was at the parade. Timmy M., my co-worker, and I were window-chatting in one of the parking lots off of Main Street.

"Here comes the parade," Timmy observed. "We'd better get out of here."

"Let's just hang out and watch," I replied. "There hasn't been a call for over an hour now."

"You can, but I'm going to head out. I don't feel like getting stuck here for two hours while waiting for the parade to pass."

After Timmy took off, I gave it a second thought and decided to take off seconds before the beginning of the parade was to pass in front of me. Timmy had joined Dave who was parked on one of the side streets off of Main Street. I thought I'd alleviate the stressful situation,

127

John "the Milkman" Wallin

as the parade was practically on top of me, and started to wave to the crowd as though I was in the parade.

"Hey John, you're a nut!" Dave bolted over the radio. I could hear Timmy laughing in the background as they were sitting window to window.

"I don't want to get stuck here for two hours either."

I was just starting to turn off Main Street onto Court Street when a couple of police officers on mountain bikes pulled along both sides of me. Dave and Timmy could still see me from where they were sitting.

"Pull over to the side of the road!" one of the officers yelled.

"Okey Dokey," I yelled back.

"Who do you think you are, the king of this parade?!" the officer yelled after I pulled over to the side of the road.

"No, but if you want you can talk to the Princess," I wisecracked. "You'll have to wait though; she's at the end of the parade."

"Another wisecrack like that and we'll haul your butt off to jail!" the second officer threatened.

"I'm sorry; I didn't want to get stuck in that parking lot where I was sitting."

"You should have been off of Main Street a half an hour ago when we put the barricades up," the first officer pointed out.

128

Scenes In The Rearview Mirror

"If we see you screwing around here again tonight, you're going to be in trouble," the second officer stated.

"No problem, it won't happen again your Highness – I mean officer."

"Hey John, from here on in you are hereby dubbed 'the Dairy Prince of Cortland County,'" Timmy radioed.

"Thanks, Timmy; I'm going to step out for a cup of coffee. I'll see you in a bit."

John "the Milkman" Wallin

Date: **October 31, 2000**
Time: **10:00 pm**
Holiday/Event: **Halloween**
Occurrence: **Hallo***weenies*

Halloween landed on a Friday night this particular year, and both the college students and the local residents were out partying in full force.

The bar rush hadn't started yet, so I decided to take a cruise down Main Street to see if I could find any stand calls. I had never seen so may people dressed up before, except maybe when I was down in New Orleans for Mardi Gras. I noticed that the costumes weren't as creative as they had been in previous years.

I pulled up in front of the Dark Horse where four people hopped into my cab. A can of whipped cream hopped in the front and three bananas hopped into the back. My taxi dome light was flickering on and off, adding to the spooky-filled night. There must have been a loose connection somewhere.

Scenes In The Rearview Mirror

"Where's the ice cream?" I asked the can of whipped cream, thinking that it would make a complete banana split.

"We're not together," the first banana revealed. "We have never seen that can of whipped cream before." I felt like I was in Wonderland with Alice.

"Where are you guys going?" I asked.

"We're going back to Randall Hall," the top banana replied.

"And where are you going?" I asked the can of whipped cream.

"We can get a real can of whipped cream and have some fun," she replied in a sexy tone of voice.

"We don't need to buy a can of whipped cream to have fun," I joked. "You already *are* the can of whipped cream."

She started to laugh and asked me to take her to Smith Towers. When I cleared with both parties, I headed back to Main Street to see what other peculiar characters I would run into. I took the college hill road back and swung over to West Court and down to Main Street. A woman covered in a bed sheet with a bunch of tears in it who hopped into my cab. She seemed like she was around fifty years old or so.

131

John "the Milkman" Wallin

"What are you supposed to be?" I inquired.

"An asshole," she replied, with a cackling laugh.

I almost said "you're an asshole all right." Instead I said, "You don't look like an asshole. All I see is a sheet with a bunch of rips in it."

"Well, I guess you have to use your imagination."

"Aaal-righty then," I mumbled. "Where are you going?"

"Take me to Palm Gardens. They are having a Halloween party."

"Hey, maybe you'll win the first prize," I sarcastically remarked.

After I dropped the asshole-- I mean the woman off -- I went back downtown to Main Street. I noticed this young college girl flagging me down in front of Woodman's Pub.

"Hop in," I yelled out of my window as I came to a stop. "That's kind of a strange costume. What are you supposed to be?"

She was carrying a fake (thank goodness) machete and she had a bunch of empty mini cereal boxes glued to her garment.

"Take a guess. What do you think I am?"

Scenes In The Rearview Mirror

I thought for a few seconds and replied, "A cereal killer?"

"That's really good," she said in a tone of amazement.

I sarcastically thought to myself, 'that was a tough one. Where do these people get their ideas?'

Soon after I dropped her off at her college dorm, I radioed, "I'm clear Dave. Do you have any calls waiting?"

"No, just go cruise the streets like you have been doing."

I pulled up in front of Brooklyn Pizza where there was a bunch of people hanging out in front, eating their pizza. Three beautiful college girls emerged from the crowd and hopped into my taxi.

"Where are you going?" I asked.

"To Alger Hall," the girl in the front seat replied.

"Where are your costumes?" I asked the three girls.

"We have them on," replied one of the two young women sitting in the back seat. "We're dressed up as ourselves."

133

John "the Milkman" Wallin

"Well let me tell you, you guys have the best costumes I've seen all night. Actually, I think the three of you resemble Fran Dresser who plays the Nanny in the sitcom *The Nanny*."

One of the girls in the back talked like the Nanny with a nasal tone in her voice and a Brooklyn accent. The other girl laughed like the Nanny, and the girl in the front seat was just as beautiful as the nanny, and looked like her as well.

"Thanks," the girl in the front seat replied after I complimented her. The two girls in the back weren't sure if laughing or talking like Fran Dresser was a good thing, so they didn't say anything at all.

"Hey, do you guys want to hear my impersonation of Edith Bunker from the sitcom *All in the Family*?"

"Sure, why not," replied the girl who looked like the Nanny.

"OK, now play the part of Archie Bunker and say, 'hey Edith, get me a beer,'" I told the girls.

"Hey Edith, get me a beer," the girl that laughed like the Nanny yelled.

"Right away, Archie," I answered in a high pitched voice, mimicking Edith. "Coming, Archie."

Scenes In The Rearview Mirror

The girl who spoke like the Nanny said, "That was really good. All you need is a wig and a dress and you'll have your costume ready to go."

"Thanks Fran, Fran, and Fran," I said to them as I dropped them off at Alger Hall. I then radioed, "I'm clear with the three Nannys, Dave."

"Pick up at Whitaker Hall. There's a girl waiting for your wonderful services," Dave returned.

I detected a slight note of sarcasm in his voice, but it was so faint I thought I'd give him the benefit of the doubt. "Thanks, Dave. That's really nice of you." I thought that maybe I was starting to get the credit that I deserved.

"I was just being sarcastic John. My delivery was off because I'm a little under the weather."

"You're a little under the influence of something," I returned, "but I'm not sure what it is."

"Yeah, yeah, just go get the call."

So up over the college hill I flew, towards Whitaker Hall. When I arrived, there was a cute little college girl, dressed up as a strawberry, waiting for me. She had strawberry blond pigtails, freckles and the cutest face I had ever seen. She also donned a green hat that

135

John "the Milkman" Wallin

was the leaf/stem part of the strawberry, and a body suit that was the actual strawberry.

"Where are you going?" I asked as she wiggled into the front seat of my cab.

"I'm going to a Halloween party at Delta Sigma Tau," she answered with a French accent.

"Is your accent real, or are you putting me on?" I returned with an English accent.

"Oui Oui, Monsieur. I'm an exchange student from France." Her voice was as cute and sweet as the outfit she was wearing.

"Wow! That's really cool! This is car fifteen; I have my cute little French strawberry, and we're going to Delta Sigma Tau."

"He must be tripping," "Bulldog" interjected over the radio. "He's starting to see things."

"Tripping?!" Dave chuckled. "It only takes him three beers to get him drunk. Can you imagine what a hit of acid would do?"

"The only acid that John has ever seen was probably in a chemistry lab in high school," Timmy (Little Indian) continued, with his own little dig. Usually, each cab driver would get their licks in one after another, in succession.

136

Scenes In The Rearview Mirror

"Who's next?" I radioed. I was finally learning -- the hard way -- that it would be easier to join 'em than to fight 'em. "Oh that's right, I forgot, there are three of you out here instead of the usual six. Thank goodness, otherwise I'd have to listen to three more jokes."

"That's all right," Dave radioed. "I'm sure the boss is sitting at home listening to his scanner with some of his own jokes."

"Along with hundreds of others who have scanners in their home." "Bulldog" stated.

"Say what you will, but I know I really do have a French Strawberry in my cab, and that's all that matters," I replied. "Don't listen to them," I told my customer. "They're all full of hot air."

Through the moonlit city streets we cruised towards Delta Sigma Tau. The wind was starting to howl and the temperatures were starting to dip to a freezing level. The dome light in my cab seemed to be getting worse, blinking twice as fast as it did when I first started my shift. I could see a guy dressed up as an electric blender, flagging me down.

"Do you mind if I pick up that dude?" I asked my little French strawberry.

"That's my boyfriend," she nervously replied. "We recently had a big fight, and I really don't want to see him. Keep on going."

"A blender, eh? That seems to be a very incompatible costume, you being a strawberry and all."

"We haven't spoken to each other for more than a week," she chuckled. "I don't think he knows what my costume is."

"Here we are my sweet little strawberry," I said as I pulled up in front of Delta Sigma Tau a few minutes later.

"Thanks cabbie, you're a sweety. "I'll call you later for my return trip home."

"I'm clear, Dave."

"Did you give your French Strawberry a lick, I mean a kiss goodbye?"

"Yep," I confidently answered. "I sprinkled some sugar on her and gave her a big fat kiss. Do you have any calls waiting?"

"Nope," Dave replied with a sigh, "I'm going to pack it in for the night. I'm not feeling too well."

"If you didn't stay out 'till all hours of the night with all of your old lady friends, you wouldn't feel so drained."

Scenes In The Rearview Mirror

"Yeah, whatever. It's all yours. I'll see you tomorrow."

"See ya later, Mr. Dave."

So I cruised down the streets to see what other peculiar characters I could find.

John "the Milkman" Wallin

Date: November 27, 2001
Time: 6:16 pm
Holiday/Event: Thanksgiving
Occurrence: Thank Goodness
For That Boy Genius

Even though Thanksgiving was quickly upon central New Yorkers, the relatively warm weather was still lingering. I was hoping that Old Man Winter got stuck somewhere up at the North Pole.

The deciduous trees still had much of their brilliant foliage. The dried up, golden corn stalks, that were bare of their corn, were still standing tall in the fields.

My boss, Tom Turkey, volunteered my services, even though I told him I didn't want to work. Like the good sport that I was, I had to suck it up. My friend and *dip*spatcher, Dave, volunteered his own services.

The city had a ghost-like feeling to it, with not a soul in sight. Business was dead, until a call came in shortly after six.

Dave was trying to give me the call, but I had my stereo up very loud.

"...Wasted away again in Margaretaville." I was singing to a Jimmy Buffet song.

140

Scenes In The Rearview Mirror

"…Searching for my lost shaker of salt… Woa!" I shouted as I came to a late stop.

"Do you always stop at a red light in the middle of the intersection?" Dave charged over the radio.

"Where the hell are you?" I returned.

"Right behind you, *behind* the cross walk, where you should be."

"Well, you don't need to be spying on me like that. It makes me nervous."

"Makes *you* nervous? What about all of the people that need to get through the green light?" Dave stated as he tried to make a rational point.

"Whatever; just let me do the driving out here. And quit sneaking up on me like that! I wish everyone out here would just worry about themselves," I mumbled to myself a moment later.

I felt like the kid of the group. Every time I turned around, the other drivers were either correcting me or catching me at something I shouldn't have been doing. Being the rebellious and non-conforming person that I was, I guess I was the kid.

"Go get the 'Children of the Corn,'" Dave commanded.

Dave took the name from the Stephen King movie, "*Children of the Corn.*" He nicknamed the kids that because they always met in an empty field just like the

141

kids did in a cornfield in the movie. I guess it was easier that way, since they could slip in and out of their homes without their parents hearing the taxi pull up. I usually picked them up after midnight while their parents were asleep, but on this particular day I picked them up much earlier.

"Where are they?" I returned.

"They are somewhere in the vicinity of the bus garage at the Cortland High School."

Ten minutes later, I rounded the high school and pulled up in front of the bus garage. I couldn't see anyone, so I beeped the horn. The lights of the garage were off and the soccer field across the way was dark.

"Hey Dave, I don't see anyone around here," I radioed.

"Give them a few minutes; they'll come out."

"Hey, John," Al yelled a few minutes later as he came out of nowhere and hopped into the front seat of my cab.

"Hey guys," I replied as Chris and Matt climbed into the back. "Where did you guys come from?"

"If we told you, we wouldn't be living up to our reputations as 'Children of the Corn,'" Chris pointed out. "We have to travel incognito, you know."

"Yeah, that's true," I replied.

"How are you doin' John?" Al asked.

Scenes In The Rearview Mirror

"I'm doing all right, except I don't want to be out here, being that it's Thanksgiving and everything."

"Why don't you just go home?" Matt suggested.

"I would, but my boss volunteered my services and I had no choice. Where are you guys going?"

"We're going to the Homer High School football field to meet some friends of ours," Al replied.

"No problem, I'll take Route 81 up to the Homer exit. That will be much faster." The Homer High School was located right off the Homer exit.

"Thanks John," Chris yelled from the back seat.

Kush—Tsh—Kish—Kish... came the sound of my stereo as I was searching for a song.

I started singing to the Beatles song, "Norwegian Wood."

"I once had a girl,
or should I say,
she once had me...
"She showed me her room
Isn't it good,
Norwegian Wood."

Al, Chris and Matt started to sing along and clap their hands to the beat.

John "the Milkman" Wallin

Several minutes and a few songs later, I noticed that I had passed the Homer exit.

"Shit!" I yelled

"What's the matter John?" Chris asked.

"I passed the Homer exit. Now we have to drive all the way to Preble to turn around." The Preble exit was around eight miles north of Homer.

"No we don't," Al reassured me. "Just go through one of the trooper turnarounds."

"That's a good idea, but they come up so fast, I might pass it."

"Well, there are three of them between Homer and Preble."

"I suppose you're going to tell me next how far the next turnaround is from here."

"No problem," Al responded like a genius reciting the gnome sequence. "We just passed the first one, and the next one is two point five miles away."

"All right, if you say so. Let me know when we get about a half of a mile from the u- turn." I kept an eye on the odometer to see just how accurate he was.

About one minute later, Al told me that I had a half of a mile to go. As I looked down at the odometer, I saw that he was right on the money. As five more tenths of a mile clicked off my odometer, there was my u-turn.

144

Scenes In The Rearview Mirror

"How does he do that?" I asked the others in the back seat as I made my u-turn and headed back towards Homer.

"He's a boy genius," Chris replied.

Five minutes later I dropped the Children of the Corn off and told them that the ride was on me.

"You the man," Matt returned.

"When you pick us up later, we'll have a bunch of Thanksgiving goodies for you." Al concluded.

"That would be great! Thanks guys. Call me when you're ready to be picked up."

I radioed to Dave to tell him that I was clear and drove to one of my favorite hiding spots where I decided to take a snooze. About a half an hour later after I fell asleep, Dave's seemingly loud voice came over the radio and woke me.

"Car Fifteen!"

"Yeah, arrgh, (cough, cough). What do you want?"

"Go get Rhonda's Bar going to the Palm Gardens."

"I can't believe these bars are open on Thanksgiving."

"You're the one who was complaining that there wasn't any business out here."

"Well there's not. And besides, I was taking a snooze."

John "the Milkman" Wallin

"Just go get the call!" Dave ordered. "And don't talk to me unless it is absolutely necessary. I'm going to take a snooze of my own."

"Whatever."

So I cruised across town to Rhonda's. When I arrived, there was a very short, petite woman waiting for me in front of the bar. It was pouring out, and she was soaking wet. She hopped into the front of my cab.

"Where are you going?" I asked. I had picked her up many times before.

"I'm going to Palm Gardens. And hurry up!" she commanded.

"How was your Thanksgiving?" I asked.

"Why, who wants to know?" she snapped back.

"I was just wondering if you spent the whole day drinking your meal." I mumbled. I could smell the alcohol as she spit every time she spoke.

"What did you say?"

"Nothing." I then radioed to Dave, "This is car fifteen; I have my fare and we're going to the Palm Gardens."

"Thanks a lot for waking me up, fifteen."

"Ooops, sorry Dave." I then sarcastically mumbled to myself, "Everyone out here is in such a great mood."

My customer then snatched my microphone which was attached to a hook on the dash panel.

146

Scenes In The Rearview Mirror

"Hey, Dave, how ya doing? Who's this new guy?" she asked as I went to grab the mic back from her.

It was a strict rule that the cabbies weren't allowed to let any of the customers talk over the radio. Sometimes, though, a rowdy customer would steal the microphone.

"Sorry Dave, she snatched the mic from me."

"You're a F@#$ing jerk," the woman blasted.

"Watch your mouth, or you'll walk!" I quickly warned. I knew where this was going because she'd been nasty to me many times before.

"Screw you, you jerk! What's your name?!"

"Sam!"

"Sam what?!" She thought she was in control of the matter at hand.

"Sam Manella."

"Well, Mr. Manella, I'm going to call your boss and get you fired."

"Go right ahead. You'd be doing me a favor. Now get out of my cab!" I demanded, as I pulled over to the side of the road.

"You're an a@#$#%, you know that?"

"So are you, now get out!"

"You wait-- just wait until I talk with your boss!" She opened the door to let herself out and slammed it so hard she lost her balance. She then spun around and landed on her butt in a puddle of water. I leaned over the seat to

147

John "the Milkman" Wallin

look out the passenger window and checked to see if she was all right. I then sped away.

"I'm clear, Dave." I purposely boomed over the radio, knowing that he was probably sleeping.

"That's good to know," Dave returned. "Thanks for waking me up…again."

"I kicked that girl out of my cab."

"That's nice," Dave calmly answered. I could sense an eruption about to happen. "Now go get the 'Children of the Corn' at the Homer High School!" he screamed.

"O'Tey!" I yelled in the microphone, sounding like Buckwheat from *The Little Rascals*.

So I picked up the children and dropped them off at their destination as promised. Al had a Thanksgiving plate all ready for me and I thanked him. The next day I found out that the woman I had kicked out of my cab had called my boss to complain. When my boss asked her for the name of the driver, she told him, Sam Manella. He immediately knew what was going on and told her, with a smile on his face, that he would take care of it.

Scenes In The Rearview Mirror

John "the Milkman" Wallin

Date: **December 24, 2001**
Time: **10:05 pm**
Holiday/Event: **Christmas Eve**
Occurrence: **The Lottery Ticket**
Scratcher-Offer

Christmas Eve was finally upon us and it was so busy that my company had eight cabs running, as opposed to the usual five or six.

The night was not only special because it was Christmas Eve, but it was special because it was Maria Burdick's birthday--at least for her and her sister, Lisa.

I was dispatched to pick up the Burdick sisters at their mother's bar (Burdick's) in McGraw.

"Hey, car fifteen," radioed my good friend and *dip*spatcher Dave.

"Yeah, what!?" I shot back. I was in a very grumpy mood because my boss, the Grinch, made me work Christmas Eve.

"Sheesh, what a grouch," Dave responded.

"Yeah, well I'm not too happy about having to work Christmas Eve.

"Not everyone can get the night off," Dave explained. "There are other drivers who have seniority over you, and you're at the bottom of the totem pole."

150

Scenes In The Rearview Mirror

"I've been at the bottom of the totem pole for four years now, and this is the fourth Christmas Eve that I've had to work! When am I going to start moving up the totem pole?"

"As soon as some of the other drivers retire," Dave chuckled. All of the other drivers, except Dave, were in their twenties and thirties. Dave was in his eighties – I mean fifties.

"I won't hold my breath," I returned.

"While you are not holding your breath, go get the Burdick sisters in McGraw.

Then on the way back through, pick up Jane Perry at Night Owls in Polkville," Dave ordered. McGraw is five miles east of Cortland and Polkville is approximately in the middle.

"Where are they going?"

"The Burdick sisters are going to the Red Dragon, and Jane is going to the Tavern."

"Okey Dokey," I replied, my mood starting to improve.

To Mcgraw I took off like Dasher, Prancer and Rudolf to pick up my beautiful girls/ When in the middle of flight, I started getting uptight when red lights behind me started to swirl/ I got so excited, I just couldn't hide it, and put the pedal to the floor/ When I looked in the rearview mirror, I could see much, much clearer; it was

John "the Milkman" Wallin

the long of the arm of the law/ So I pulled to one side, with my bruised ego and pride, and the officer said to slow down, and that he'd see me around/ And I suddenly knew what Christmas meant/ It was time for good will, and not for quotas to be filled, and a break from the law--Heaven sent.

"Car fifteen; did you get your call yet?" Dave radioed.

"No I haven't, Dave."

"What's the hold up?"

"I got pulled over by a really nice deputy sheriff."

"You must be on something," Dave wise cracked. "I've never heard you speak so highly of the police before."

"Well you know, it's Christmas Eve, and it's time for peace on Earth."

"Hmm, I guess you *can* teach old dog new tricks," Dave mumbled to himself.

I then entered the little village of McGraw, and pulled up in front of the post office where the Burdick sisters were standing.

"Hey girls," I greeted, as they hopped into the back seat of my cab.

"How are you?" Lisa returned.

"I'm doing just fine," I replied. "I was in a real rotten mood, but now I'm much better."

"That's good," Maria responded.

Scenes In The Rearview Mirror

"Where are you girls going?"

"We are going to the Red Dragon on Tompkins Street," Lisa replied. Lisa was a bartender there, and her sister bartended at the Tavern on South Main Street.

"Okey Dokey. I have to pick up a fare at Night Owls on the way, if that's OK."

"No problem," Maria replied. "Who are you picking up?" Between her and her sister, they just about knew everyone in Cortland.

"I'm picking up Jane Perry. Do you know her?"

"Oh sure," Lisa replied. "She frequents the Red Dragon where I bartend."

Five minutes later I pulled up in front of Night Owls and out came Jane, raring to go.

"Thanks, cabbie," Jane said as she hopped into the front seat.

"No problem. Where are you going?" Even though I knew where they were going, I thought I should ask just in case they changed their mind.

"To the Tavern," Jane answered. "Can you stop by the convenience store first? I want to buy some lottery tickets."

"No problem, it's on the way anyway."

"Have you won any big ones lately, Jane?" Maria asked. Jane was well known for her big winnings on scratch off tickets.

153

John "the Milkman" Wallin

"Not really. The last time I won anything to speak of was six months ago when I won $777.00 on Lucky 7s."

"Wow, that's pretty good, "I commended.

"That's nothing," Jane boasted. "I won $2,000.00 six months before that and $5,000.00 a year before that."

"No kidding. What is your strategy?"

"None, really. I guess I'm just lucky."

A few minutes later, I pulled up in front of the convenience store where Jane went in to buy her lottery tickets. When she got back into the car, she started scratching them all off. When she got to her sixth and final ticket, she scratched it off and started to scream, "Oh my GOD!"

"What's the matter?!" Lisa yelled back.

"Check this Lisa, and tell me I'm not dreaming." She handed the scratched off ticket to Lisa in the back.

Lisa looked at the ticket and her eyes looked like they were going to pop out of her head. "Hey John, turn the dome light on, will you?"

"OK," I replied

"Maria, please look at this and tell me I'm not mistaken!" Lisa yelled. Maria looked at both Jane and Lisa as though they were off their rockers.

"Oh my GOD!" Maria yelled as she looked at the ticket.

"What the heck is going on?" I asked.

154

Scenes In The Rearview Mirror

Maria then handed me the ticket and told me to check it out. I pulled over and examined the ticket.

"Holy moley!" I yelled. "It's a $7,777.00 winner!" It was a Lucky 7s ticket, Jane's favorite. "I can't believe it!"

The girls started hugging one another in jubilation. I then gave the ticket back to Jane, and a few minutes later we pulled up in front of the Tavern.

"Here you go, cabbie," Jane gladly offered. "Here is the fare and an extra hundred dollars for you. Here is another ten dollars for Lisa and Maria's fare."

"Thanks, Jane!" Lisa yelled as Jane hopped out of the cab.

I proceeded to the Red Dragon where I dropped the two beautiful Burdick sisters off.

"Hey John, did you drop the Burdick sisters off yet?"

"Yeah Dave, I'm clear at the Red Dragon."

"Go get 57 Groton Ave. There's a college student that needs to go to Wilson Farms."

"I'm after it, Ole Grey Mighty One."

Five minutes later I arrived at my destination and picked the college dude up.

"I have 57 Groton, Dave, and we're going to "The Farm"... Dave?...Oh Dave?" So I said to myself, 'Self? What does one have to do to get an answer around here?'

155

John "the Milkman" Wallin

I radioed to myself: "I guess he must have stepped out for a cup of java."

"Hop in, dude," I yelled through the opened window of my taxi-cab.

"Thanks, cabbie."

"Where are you going?"

"I'm going to Wilson Farms. Can you hurry? I had to be there five minutes ago."

"No problem," I chuckled. "What's your name?"

"Eric; what's yours?"

"John."

"Nice to meet you."

"Nice to meet you as well. I can't believe you have to work on Christmas Eve," I empathetically stated.

"Yeah, I can't believe it either. A lot of my fellow employees are out sick, and they called me in."

"That stinks. How come you didn't go home with all of the rest of the students?"

"My boss told me to stick around just in case."

"Hey, would you like a cookie? Some woman gave me a whole tin of them. I picked her up at a Christmas party and she told me that she was on a diet and didn't want to gain a

hundred pounds--if you know what I mean."

"Yeah. You could stand to lose a few pounds yourself--if you know what I mean," he joked.

156

Scenes In The Rearview Mirror

"Well, you know, I have to get dressed up this Christmas as Santa Claus for my own Christmas party."

"Well you definitely fit the part, but I think your going to have to be fitted for a costume. Don't you think?"

"Yeah, I'm going to have to be fitted with a body suit because I'm not fat enough to wear a normal costume. Maybe when I have my party, I'll eat the rest of these cookies and I'll gain enough weight to actually be as fat as Santa Claus."

"You're a riot, John, you know that?"

"Wait until you read my book on all my taxi adventures."

"I can't wait."

"Well here we are, Eric."

"How much is that, Mr. cabbie man?"

"Don't worry about it; it's on the house--I mean cab."

"You know, I think I'm going to take you down to New York City with me tomorrow, and wrap you up in a huge box to put under the Christmas tree. That way my parents could open it up and meet you."

"That would be great! Where would you like to meet?" I chuckled. "I'm only kidding."

"I know. Have a nice Christmas, John. I hope to see you when I get back from my winter break."

John "the Milkman" Wallin

"That would be great! I'll see ya. Have a happy Christmas."

"Adiós, amigo!"

"Are you clear yet, John?" Dave radioed a few moments later.

"Yeah Dave, I'm clear," I replied, feeling humble.

"Okey Dokey. Get the scooper out and sweep the streets for any would-be riders."

"OK, Mr. Dave."

"Hey, John."

"Yes?"

"Merry Christmas."

"You too, man."

Taxi Jams

The first year of my five-year career as a taxi-cab driver was one of the craziest years of my life. Every time I turned around, I was getting into some kind of trouble. It got to the point where every night, at the beginning of my shift, I would wonder what crazy thing was going to happen to me.

Many times when a situation would arise, I would become totally stressed out and unfocused. Things would start to *snowball* from there. Here are some of the more interesting predicaments that I got myself into. I hope you find them as funny as I do *now*.

John "the Milkman" Wallin

Date: October 13, 1997
Time: 9:51 pm
Holiday/Event: Bow Season
Occurrence: A Ten Point Rack,
a Thousand Dollar Wreck

They say that you should keep your sense of humor when the chips are down. I find that this is a good habit to get into, but almost impossible to stick to.

Bow season was in full swing in Central New York, and it was time to greet those friendly faces on the side of the road—that is, the faces of deer, not the hunters.

I was heading down Route 281 in Cortland when a call was given to me by my *dip*spatcher, Dave. He was dispatching from his cab.

"Car fifteen; go get the 281 Bowling Alley. Billy the floor buffer needs a ride home." Billy waxed and buffed the floors of local business' and bowling alleys for a living.

"No problem. I'm on my way, Ole Grey Mighty One."

"Don't be a wise guy; just go get the call!"

I couldn't resist the urge to continue busting on Dave. "Hey Dave, they say that the women like guys with grey hair."

Scenes In The Rearview Mirror

"Yeah, they like guys who are bald too," Dave returned, making fun of my receding hairline. "Now go get the call!"

"Whatever. They also say that a bald man's head is a solar panel for a sex machine!"

"I can tell it's going to be one of those nights," Dave mumbled.

"What's that?"

"Nothing," he said. "Please go get the call." Dave wasn't in his usual joking mood.

So down the road I went to pick up Billy the floor waxer. When I arrived at the parking lot of the 281 Bowling Alley, I noticed Billy's van parked on the side of the building. I went into the entrance, and there he was sitting at the bar talking with the pretty bartender. I motioned to him to come out.

"How the heck are ya, Billy?" I asked, as we walked out of the bowling alley towards my cab. "Are you going home?"

"No, take me to the Armadillo. I need a drink," he replied in his usual gruff tone of voice.

"No problem," I said as I sped away. "Rough day on the job?"

"Yeah, what else is new? Hey! Watch out for that skunk in the road!" Billy yelled.

161

John "the Milkman" Wallin

"Don't worry, I've never hit a skunk before," I reacted as I swerved to miss the smelly varmint. "And I don't plan on ever hitting one either."

"That's good, because I don't feel like walking into the Armadillo smelling like a skunk."

"I've hit just about every kind of animal you can think of," I continued. "I've hit a deer, a rabbit, a fox and a dog. I even hit a camel one night."

"A camel?" Billy incredulously replied. "I find that hard to believe."

"Yep, it was lying in the middle of the road, and it was still smoking."

"Very funny," he replied with a sarcastic laugh. "Speaking of cigarettes, do you have one I can bum off you?"

"No, I don't smoke."

Just then, WHACK – SLAM! One of those friendly faces had come wandering into the road and met up with the front end of my cab.

"Are you all right, Billy?"

"Yeah, I can't believe that deer just popped out of nowhere!"

"It looks like a buck to me," I guessed. "I wonder how many points it is."

"I don't know," Billy replied. "Let's check it out."

162

Scenes In The Rearview Mirror

We climbed out of the cab and walked around to the front. I noticed that the grille and the front part of the hood were smashed in. The passenger side headlight was also broken.

"It's a ten-pointer!" Billy exclaimed.

I turned to the deer and examined it. "Wow! Look at the size of that rack! My friends would love to hang *that* on their walls."

"Yeah, that's a lot of venison too," Billy remarked.

My friends have a 45-acre piece of land in Freeville, five miles west of Cortland. For the most part they live off the land. They hunt game throughout the year, whether it's deer, duck, pheasant or crazy rabbit season. They grow their own vegetables, and raise pigs and turkeys for slaughter. With all the hunting relics, real and replicas, their home and land looks like something from the mid 1800's.

"I wonder if there's any rope in my cab."

"Why's that?" Billy asked.

"I'm thinking of tying it on the luggage rack on the roof and bringing it over to my friend's house."

After I found some rope, we lifted the buck onto the roof and tied it down as securely as possible.

"I'll drop you off first, Billy. Then I'll take a quick trip over to my friends' place. Thanks for the help."

John "the Milkman" Wallin

"No problem, John. What are you going to tell your dispatcher?"

"I don't know," I replied as I gave him a rogue's grin, "but I'll think of something."

A few minutes later, I dropped Billy, "the floor shiner," off at the Armadillo, and told him the ride was on me for helping out.

"I'll see you, Billy. Have a nice night," I called to him as he exited the cab.

"Good luck," he replied. He turned and walked into the bar.

I picked up my microphone and radioed to Dave, "Hey Dave, this is car fifteen; I'm clear, and you're not going to believe this."

"What's that?"

I decided that bluntness was the best approach. "I hit a deer."

"Oh, great!" Dave exclaimed. "How much damage was done to the cab?"

"The grille and the front part of the hood are smashed in, and the right headlight is broken," I reported.

"That must have been a pretty large deer," Dave guessed.

"Yeah, it's a ten-pointer," I confirmed. "Well, I have to step out now to take care of some business."

164

Scenes In The Rearview Mirror

"We're kind of busy out here. Where are you stepping out at?"

"I have the deer tied to the rack on the roof of my cab and I was thinking of taking it over to my friends' place."

"You're something else, you know that?!" Dave blasted. "You should have left it in the road. We're not out here to play games, you know!"

"Well, we're not out here to hit any game either!" I shot back.

"Just hurry up!"

"Sheesh, what a grouch," I mumbled to myself.

So away I went back across 281 heading towards Freeville where my friends Jason Wood and John May lived. All of a sudden, as I sped up at the 55 mph speed zone, my hood flew open, smashing my windshield and shifting the deer on the roof.

"I can't believe this!" I cried. "Why me?!" I could only see between the hood and the body of the car. I gradually pulled off to the side of the road, using the double yellow line as a guide. I took a deep breath and picked up the microphone, "Hey, Dave."

"Yeah, John?" Dave sighed. "What now?"

"You're not going to believe this."

"I'd believe anything with you."

"The wind blew my hood open."

165

John "the Milkman" Wallin

"No kidding," Dave sarcastically stated. "Is that all?"

"No," I admitted. "The windshield is smashed."

Dave was furious now. "Didn't you check to see if the hood was secure after you saw all the damage from hitting the deer?!" he thundered.

"Uh, no. I didn't think of that. Hey, can you come up here? I need your help," I pleaded. "The hood also slammed into the deer and it's hanging halfway off now."

"OK, Stanley," he seethed, imitating Oliver Hardy from the famous comedy team *Laurel and Hardy*, "I'll go get my pickup truck."

Dave then parked his cab and came up 281 to help me out, leaving only two drivers to work the city.

Scenes In The Rearview Mirror

John "the Milkman" Wallin

Date: **December 16, 1997**
Time: **11:52 pm**
Holiday/Event: ---
Occurrence: **Snow Bank**

It was a cold and blustery night in the middle of December. We were in the middle of a nor'easter which was dropping its payload on the east coast, from the Mid-Atlantic States to the northern tip of Maine.

Most of the college students were safe and warm in the confines of their dorm rooms. There weren't many town folk that were willing to brave the elements either. As a matter of fact, the only people that were out were the ones that were working at their places of employment. Most of those places, such as the bars and restaurants, were closing early.

A call was given to me to pick up a dude at a bar called the Rusty Nail. He had just finished his shift and he needed to go home. He lived about five miles or so outside the city, up Pendleton Street Extension.

"Hey John, go pick up Dudley at the Crusty Snail," Dave radioed. We use to make our own names up for each bar.

168

Scenes In The Rearview Mirror

"What was that?" I replied. My mind was still on the beautiful college girl that I had just dropped off a half hour earlier.

"What are you, deaf? Go get the Crusty Snail!"

"More like blind, with love, that is. I'm on my way," I sighed.

As I made my way (slowly, but surely) up Route 281 where the Rusty Nail was located, I saw a jeep off to the side of the road. It was half submerged in a snow bank. The driver was standing on the side of the road, covered with snow up to his waist.

I slowly came to a stop in the middle of the road. "Do you want me to call a tow truck for you?" I shouted.

"No thanks, my friend is coming with his pickup truck."

"OK." I shook my head and mumbled to myself, "I can't believe what some people get themselves into."

I then started making my way again towards the Rusty Nail. When I pulled into the parking lot of the restaurant/bar, there was one car being jump started by another, and another car that was totally disabled.

I noticed Dudley talking to the owner of the bar and called to him, "Hey, Dudley! Are you ready to go?"

"I'm coming." He hopped into the back seat with his usual doggy bag and six-pack of beer.

John "the Milkman" Wallin

"Nice night out," I sarcastically remarked. "Are you going home?"

"You've got that right. I think I'll batten down the hatch for a few days when I get there."

"Not a bad idea," I commended. "I'd like to be stranded for a few days with that beautiful college girl that I just dropped off earlier."

I made my way through the city, up to Pendelton Street Extension. "Take it easy up this road," Dudley warned. "It's really slippery."

As my thoughts were on other things, Dudley grew concerned and tried to get my attention.

"Did you hear me? Take it easy going up this road!" he reiterated.

"Uh, what?" I finally replied, coming out of my daze. "Oh yeah."

"Pay attention!" he yelled.

"Yeah, yeah, whatever," I replied, nonchalantly.

As we got to the top of the hill where Pendleton Street intersects with Starr Road, I started losing momentum. The more I accelerated, the more I slid towards the side of the road.

"Oh, great," I mumbled under my breath.

"What was that?" Dudley asked nervously.

"I can't seem to quite make it to the top!" I replied.

170

Scenes In The Rearview Mirror

"Watch it!" Dudley cried as my cab slid off the road, into a six-foot embankment. Snow drifted about, as my adrenaline reached the panic level. I then took stock of the situation. I couldn't help but think of the guy I had seen earlier in a similar position.

"Are you all right, Dudley?"

"Yeah, I'm just dandy," he sarcastically replied. "I told you to be careful!"

I looked in the rearview mirror and noticed he looked a bit piqued and yellow at the gills.

"This is car fifteen, Dave."

"Go ahead, John."

"You're never going to believe this, but I'm stuck at the top of Pendleton Street right where it intersects with Starr Road. Can you get another driver up here to take Dudley home?"

"For some strange reason, this doesn't surprise me. Yeah, I'll get Tim (Little Indian) up there as soon as possible."

"Call a tow truck too, Dave. We have to get this car out of here before the heavy snowfall covers the rest of it."

"Yeah, the boss will just love that," Dave returned. "Just another unnecessary expense. I'll have to get my pick-up truck and pull you out myself. Just hang on."

John "the Milkman" Wallin

I turned to Dudley, and asked, "Why don't you come up and sit in the front with me?"

"For some strange reason I feel safer sitting back here," Dudley snidely replied.

"Suit yourself," I said casually, as though these types of situations were usual everyday occurrences.

Just then, 'Little Indian's' voice sounded over the radio. "John, where are you? Never mind, I see you. Well, half of you anyway. Tell Dudley to get out of the car, I'm right here."

Since the back half of the cab was totally submerged, Dudley had to climb over the front seat and use the front passenger door to get out. "Sorry, Dudley," I called.

"Hey, no problem; It was the most exciting cab ride that I've ever had," he sarcastically replied.

"Dave is on his way up, John," Little Indian radioed.

"Tell him to hurry! It's getting cold out here!" I shivered.

"No problem. Would you like me to bring you back some hot soup?" 'Little Indian' asked as he was getting a kick out of the whole thing.

"Bunch of wise guys," I mumbled to myself. "Just hurry up!"

Ten minutes passed with no sign of Dave. I was starting to get worried, when Little Indian's voice came across my radio once again.

172

Scenes In The Rearview Mirror

"Hey John, I'm clear. Is Dave there yet?"

"No," I groused. "Where the hell is he?"

"I'm sure he's coming. Maybe he had trouble digging his pick-up truck out of the snow." Little Indian was silent for a moment. "Hey, John."

"Yeah, Little Indian?"

"You're not going to believe this."

"That's my line," I returned. What is it?"

"Dudley pissed his pants and he's really pissed off."

"Oh, well," I sighed. "At least he's now at home where it's nice and warm."

Dave finally pulled up with his pick-up truck. "How ya doing, Snow Bank?" he asked, chuckling at his new nickname for me.

"Oh, just great," I replied in a frustrated tone. The jokes began to fly over the radio faster than the snow falling from the sky. 'Just wait until they all find out that Dudley pissed his pants,' I silently moped. 'I'll never live it down.'

From that day on, every time Dudley called my cab company he asked for someone else.

173

John "the Milkman" Wallin

> **Date:**   **January 5, 1998**
> **Time:**   **10:11 pm**
> **Holiday/Event:**   **Duck Hunting Season**
> **Occurrence:**   **Wacky Duck and Wingnut**

I've dealt with some pretty whacked out people before, but these two took the cake.

"Wacky Duck" got his nickname from being a duck hunter. And since he was somewhat wacky to begin with, the name fit.

"Wingnut," on the other hand, was a mechanic in addition to being a cab driver. He got his nickname from his last name Winger, and the fact that he had a few nuts and bolts missing. But I guess we all did, to a degree.

One night I was dispatched to pick up a couple from a local department store outside the city. They must have called Wacky Duck and Wingnut's cab company as well. People would often call more than one company because they were in a hurry. They'd wind up taking the first cab that got there, and this in turn would cause conflicts between the different companies. It also caused what we called taxi wars, sometimes lasting for months.

After I picked up the couple at the department store, I noticed Wacky Duck had pulled into the parking lot. From the look on his face I could tell that he thought I

Scenes In The Rearview Mirror

was deliberately trying to steal his fare. He followed me all the way to West Main Street where I dropped the couple off, and pulled alongside my car.

"You have some nerve stealing my fare!" Wacky Duck charged.

"I didn't steal your fare," I replied with a mischievous smile on my face and a patronizing tone in my voice. I was trying to further instigate a situation that was going to get out of hand anyway.

"You sure as hell did!" Wacky Duck insisted. He then radioed, "Hey Wingnut, I have John and we're down here on West Main."

"OK," Wingnut returned, "I'll be there in two minutes. Don't let him out of your sight!"

A few minutes later, there was Wingnut, pulling in front of me, bumper to bumper, to help box me in with Wacky Duck. Wacky Duck backed up and pulled behind me, bumper to bumper, as well. They both hopped out of their cabs and walked over to me.

"What the hell are you guys up to?!" I yelled.

"You stole our call!" Wingnut screamed.

"Did not!" I returned

"Did too!"

"Not!"

"Too!"

"Not!"

175

John "the Milkman" Wallin

"Too!"

Things were starting to get hot, sweaty and totally ridiculous.

"You guys are really something else, you know that?!" I felt like Andy in Mayberry, reprimanding Barney and Floyd.

"Car fifteen;" Dave Churchill (D.C.) radioed, "Are you clear with your call yet?"

"Yeah, D.C., but I'm in a bit of a jam right now."

"What's going on?"

"Wacky Duck and Wingnut are accusing me of stealing a call from them. They have me boxed in on West Main."

"I'll be right over," D.C. impatiently replied.

Wacky Duck and Wingnut knew D.C. was a sixty-five year old ex-marine who had a hot temper. He had a reputation of standing his ground when push came to shove.

"Well, I think we've gotten our point across here, don't you Wacky Duck?!" Wingnut exclaimed. He heard D.C.'s response.

"Yeah, I think our work here is done," Wacky Duck replied. "We'll be keeping an eye on you, John. Don't ever let this happen again."

"Whatever, boys. Have a nice night," I replied, a patronizing tone in my voice.

176

Scenes In The Rearview Mirror

When D.C. arrived, I told him what happened.

"OK, John, that's cool."

"Where are you going?" I asked as D.C. started to take off.

"To take care of business."

"Oh boy," I mumbled to myself. "Wacky Duck and Wingnut are in for it now."

A half hour later D.C. radioed, "Hey John, did any calls come in while I was gone?"

"No D.C.," I replied. "So what happened? You didn't hurt them, did you?"

"No, I just gave them a few lessons on etiquette and how to act like men instead of children."

"Good job!" I commended. "Do you think it did any good?"

"Probably not. You know those two; they'll never change."

"That's true. Hey, can I buy you a cup of coffee?"

"Sure, why not," D.C. replied. "We deserve a coffee break after that fiasco."

John "the Milkman" Wallin

Date: **January 21, 1998**
Time: **9:44 pm**
Holiday/Event: ---
Occurrence: **Snow Cliff**

One very snowy, frigid and blustery evening I was cruising in my cab down Main Street. It was snowing so hard that I couldn't see ten feet in front of me.

As I passed Friday's Neighborhood, a local college bar, I caught a glimpse of a regular customer of mine, Jim, who was flagging me down. I jammed on my breaks and slid about thirty feet past the bar and Jim. As I looked into the rearview mirror, I could see Jim with his arms up in the air. Luckily, there were no cars coming the other way because I slid right through the red light past the intersection. I checked my rearview mirror again to see if any cars were behind me, and backed up all the way back to Friday's Neighborhood. Jim jumped back on to the sidewalk so he wouldn't get run over.

I wondered if one could get two tickets for going through the same light twice. I don't think it's ever happened before in motor vehicle history. Anyway, as I pulled over – backwards – to where Jim was standing, a cop passed me going towards the intersection. Since there

Scenes In The Rearview Mirror

weren't any other cars on the road, and it was snowing so hard, he just looked at me and shook his head.

I guess I could have gotten three tickets: one for going through the red light in the first place, another for backing through the same red light in the second place and another ticket for backing down Main Street the wrong way, since it's a one way street. Phew, I'm getting exhausted just telling you about this.

Anywho, when Jim apprehensively hopped into my cab, he asked me if I could get him home—in one piece, that is. I told him, "Sure, no problem." I then radioed the call into my fellow cabbie Steve (The Man) Dumond who was dispatching from the office since business was so slow.

Jim lived in Marathon, some fifteen miles south of Cortland. He came into Cortland once a week, usually on a Saturday night, to party at his favorite bars. He usually went back home to Marathon after the bars closed at 2:00 in the morning. It was very difficult to get through to the different cab companies, since they were always so busy. He never bothered to call any of them. He would just flag down the first cab that would come along. For some strange reason though, I won the prize at least seventy-five percent of the time. Jim didn't mind because we got along very well. I didn't mind because I enjoyed his company.

John "the Milkman" Wallin

And my pocket didn't mind either, as the fare was twenty-five dollars.

"Nice weather we're having, eh?" I sarcastically stated, as Jim hopped in the front of my cab.

"Yeah, I think I'm going to retire early and move to Florida." Jim was in the construction business.

"How have you been doin' otherwise, Jim?"

"Not bad," Jim returned with a laugh. He always laughed at the things that weren't funny and didn't laugh at the things that were. How have *you* been?"

"Not bad, except for that drunken idiot I had in my cab earlier."

"Oh yeah, what happened?" Jim asked with a laugh.

"This 6'5" college student who got into my cab was drunk and very obnoxious."

"Oh yeah?" Jim laughed again.

"What's so funny?" I asked.

"Nothing; just my usual stress-relieving laugh. So what did you do?"

"I stopped my taxi and very firmly told him to get out."

"Oh yeah? What happened then?"

"He got out."

"That's it?"

"Yep. It doesn't take much. You have to be in control of the situation, and show them who 'the boss' is."

180

Scenes In The Rearview Mirror

"Yeah, I guess." Jim responded with another laugh.

"Hey, Jim."

"What?"

"How much does it cost for a pirate to have his ears pierced?"

"I don't know, how much?"

"A buccaneer."

"That's pretty funny," Jim responded without laughing.

"So how come you're not laughing?"

"I don't know, that's just the way I am."

"Oh."

A few minutes later I started to pull up in Jim's driveway, which led to his house. The driveway was about eighty feet long.

"Here you go, Jim. I don't think I can make it any further, so I'll let you off here." There was at least a foot of snow that had fallen since Jim left his house eight hours earlier.

"No problem," Jim returned. "Here's the twenty-five dollars, and a five dollar tip for you."

"Thanks, as always, Jim. I'll see you next time."

"Yep; probably next week."

Jim hopped out of my cab and made his way through the two feet of snow towards his house. When he got about twenty feet away, the snow got deeper and deeper

181

and Jim sunk down further and further. As he tried to lift his legs up to tread the snow, he fell forward, face first.

"Are you all right, Jim?!" I yelled. "Hey, Jim!"

I heard a muffled voice saying "Help! Get me out of here!"

"Here we go again" I mumbled to myself. "I have to play the baby sitter." I then yelled, "I'm coming Jim! Hang loose!"

I walked over to him, and it was like the blind leading the blind. I reached out to grab his arm and tried to pull him out. I then fell in the three feet of snow with him. This re-positioned him, where his face wasn't buried in the snow anymore. We both started to laugh hysterically.

"This is the first time I heard you laugh, Jim, when something funny has happened."

"Yeah, well, there's a first time for everything."

I thought to myself, 'At least I accomplished one thing tonight: Getting Jim to laugh when something is funny.' After a few minutes, we both managed to help each other out of the snow.

"I'll wait until you get in the door Jim, just in case you fall in again," I yelled as he took the last twenty or so steps to his safe abode.

Jim started to laugh again. "Thanks man, I'll see you next week."

Scenes In The Rearview Mirror

When I got to back Cortland, Steve 'the Man' Dumond, gave me a call to pick up Space Trailer Park. When I arrived there, I noticed that the roadway that led to the three different levels hadn't been plowed. I thought to myself 'Oh boy, here we go.' As I started up the hill, I could barely get any traction. I had to go real slow so I wouldn't start to slide, but as I got towards the top I started to slide towards the cliff.

The more I tried keeping my cab from going off the road, the further it drifted into the pile of snow and then down the hill. I panicked, wondering if there was anything I could do to keep from furthering my reputation for driving into snow banks. The situation continued to snowball, and I only sank further and further down the hill as I tried to figure out how I was going to 'dig myself out of this one.' I just wanted to get the hell out of there.

Finally, I gave up and reached for the microphone of my radio. "This is car fifteen; you're not going to believe this, but I'm hanging off the side of a cliff!"

"For some strange reason, I don't find that hard to believe," Steve replied. "Where are you stuck?"

"I'm at the top of Space Trailer Park, hanging off the side of the hill. I'm sliding further and further down to the bottom of the cliff!"

183

John "the Milkman" Wallin

"You've got to be kidding!" Steve exclaimed. "I'll be there with my truck to see if I can pull you out!"

I tried to keep the panic out of my voice. "Uh, I hope you have a chain long enough because it's at least thirty feet to the bottom!"

"Just hang on, Snow Bank. I'll be right up." I could hear a chuckle in his voice.

"Hey Snow Bank, how many times does this make?!" Dave, my usual dispatcher, radioed.

"Very funny, Dave," I sullenly replied.

A short time later, I had reached the bottom of my descent, down the thirty-foot plus embankment. I looked to the top of the hill and spotted Steve's rugged silhouette peering down at me as he was waving his arms.

"How the hell are you going to get yourself out of this mess?!" he exclaimed as he shook his head.

I held my head in my hand. "I don't know. I just don't know."

Scenes In The Rearview Mirror

John "the Milkman" Wallin

Date: **February 9, 1998**
Time: **4:21 pm**
Holiday/Event: ---
Occurrence: **Rotten Rotty**

I've been in many *sticky* situations before, but there is something about coming face to face with a hungry and angry rottweiler that doesn't compare to anything else.

Getting stuck in a snow bank, getting stuck in an elevator, or even being mugged doesn't compare to the helpless feeling of being cornered by a rotty. And let me tell you, having a window between us didn't help any.

"Hey, Snow bank," Dave radioed, "Are you out there, oh, Snow Bank?"

"He's probably stuck in some pile of snow," 'Little Indian' joked.

"I'll tell you what, wise guys, I'll just go home and you can take care of business out here yourselves." I wasn't in any mood for their wise cracks.

"Relax," "Little Indian" returned.

"Go get the trailer park at the end of Creol Road in Homer," Dave ordered. "It's number 30; the fifteenth trailer on the right."

"I'm after it," I returned. "Where are they going?"

Scenes In The Rearview Mirror

"To Greek Peak Ski Resort where there's five feet of snow," Dave busted. "Just be careful, and don't get stuck."

"I can see it's going to be one of those nights," I mumbled to myself.

So up and away to Creol Road I slid, through all the pot-hole-filled streets. When I got there, I had to drive real slowly since all the holes on the dirt road were filled with about eight inches of slush.

"You'd think that they would pave this dirt road up here, or at least fill in all of the holes," I radioed as I pulled up in front of the trailer. "I'm sitting in front of trailer number 30."

Ten minutes went by and no one came out. "Hey Dave, there's no one coming out."

"Just leave it," Dave returned, "and come on back."

"Great! My car just conked out and I can't get it started. It must be that loose battery cable again."

I got out of the car to open the hood and check my battery cables when I noticed this huge rottweiler charging towards me from the back yard of number 30.

"Shit!" I yelled as I jumped back into my cab. "Nice doggy."

He looked real mean with his seemingly saber tooth-like mandibles sticking out. His steamy breath fogged up part of the window with his tongue sticking in and out

John "the Milkman" Wallin

like a huge Heila Monster. I beeped the horn to see if that would scare him away.

"This is car fifteen, Dave."

"Yeah, John. Did you get your car started?"

"No, not really, but I have this huge rottweiler staring me in the face."

"Maybe he's hungry," 'Little Indian' cracked.

"Hey Dave, you'd better get up here. I can't get the car started and this beast won't let me out of the car."

"Well, it will be at least an hour," Dave returned. I could hear one of his customers chuckling in the background. "It's getting real busy here in the city."

"Are you crazy?!" I blasted. "I can't stay up here trapped with this monster growling at me for an hour." I beeped the horn again, thinking that maybe someone in one of the trailers would hear me.

"Hey John," Little Indian broke in, "At least you're not stuck in a snow bank."

"You're a riot 'Little Indian,'" I barked. "Just wait until one of you guys get into a jam and ask for my help. Just wait!"

"Arghh, growl, ruff, ruff" the rotty barked.

"Oh shut up, you mutt!" I then beeped the horn once again. I mumbled to myself, "How the heck am I going to get myself out of this one? I'd rather be stuck in the

188

largest snow bank in New York then have to look down the throat of this animal's mouth."

I opened the window about an inch or so to see if I could calm the beast down. "Nice doggy. Good dog. Hey, if you let me go, I'll bring you back a nice thick steak that I have in my refrigerator."

"Rrrr," the dog growled. "Ruff, Ruff."

"I guess not," I replied.

I noticed that the dog kept on sticking his tongue in and out of the thin opening of my window. I thought that maybe if I shut the window real fast, I could catch his tongue in it. Then I could exit the passenger side of my cab, open the hood and reconnect the battery cable. I knew that I'd have to time it just right. The first couple of times I tried it, my timing was way off, but on the third time I was triumphant. As I heard the dog start to whimper in pain, I quickly headed towards the passenger side to open the door and make my exit. To my disbelief the rotten rotty was already there to greet me.

"I guess it pays to have a slippery, slithering tongue," I discouragingly mumbled to myself. "Hey Dave are you there?"

"Yes, John. I thought you'd be dinner by now."

"Very funny. I'm going to need your help up here."

John "the Milkman" Wallin

"Relax John," Little Indian interjected. "I'm sure you'll figure something out. After all you've had plenty experience in getting yourself out of all of these jams."

"Rrrr!"

"Sounds like the dog is becoming agitated," Dave radioed.

"No, that was me," I returned. "I'm getting pissed off." You could hear "Little Indian" and Dave chuckling over the radio while they continued making their wisecracks.

I started looking around, trying to figure out what I was going to do next. I noticed that I still had my half of a Bar-BQ chicken that I had bought earlier but didn't have time to eat. I thought to myself that 'there is always a reason for everything.' I opened the passenger side window real fast and winged the chicken as far as I could. The dog went for it! I hopped out of my cab, opened the hood and reconnected the cable. "That'll fix ya, you dirty mutt." I could see the dog chomping on the chicken and eyeballing me at the same time. He was probably trying to decide which would taste better, me or the chicken. He suddenly made his decision and started to take off back towards me and my cab.

"Shit!" I yelled once again. I quickly jumped back in my taxi, turned the key, and away I went.

When I reached the end of the dirt road about a hundred yards away, I hit this huge pot hole filled with

Scenes In The Rearview Mirror

slush and my cab stalled out again. I tried to restart it, with no success. As I looked in the rearview mirror, I could see the rottwieler charging after me once again.

"Shit! Here we go again." I jumped out of the cab, opened my hood and reconnected the cable. I turned around and headed towards the opened door of my cab. I jumped in and slammed the door with the charging rotty about ten feet away.

"You can't outsmart me, dumb dog," I smirked. "Hey Dave, I'm on my way back."

"I was just on my way up," he jokingly replied. "How did you get yourself out of this mess?! Never mind; I don't want to know."

"Don't worry, I'm not going to tell you because maybe someday you'll be in the same situation and you'll need *my* assistance."

John "the Milkman" Wallin

Date: **February 21, 1998**
Time: **7:12 pm**
Holiday/Event: **---**
Occurrence: **Snow-dazed**

Here we go again. It was snowing so hard that you couldn't see ten feet ahead of yourself. Two drivers called in sick and we had only three drivers, opposed to the usual five or six. Being the hot dog, moneymaking, go-getter that I am, I got myself into another one of my snow bank-taxi jams.

I was dispatched to pick up Rob and Mike, a couple of employees at Price Stopper Grocery Store.

"Car fifteen."

"Yeah Dave."

"Go pick up Price Stopper. There are a couple of employees who need a ride."

"Well, I'll try to pick the store up, but it's kind of heavy."

"Yeah, whatever," Dave responded. "Just go get the call, and hurry up. We're getting backed up on calls!"

"Don't worry about me, when there's money to be made, I always hustle."

Five minutes later, I pulled into the parking lot of Price Stopper. I could see Rob and Mike waiting at the

192

Scenes In The Rearview Mirror

entrance. I considerably increased my speed to hustle along and I quickly learned how slippery the parking lot was. At around 40 mph, I started sliding to the left of the lot where there were several huge piles of snow. Of course the way my luck usually went, I was uncontrollably heading for the largest one. It was as big as a house. Ten seconds after I smashed into the mountain of snow, I realized what had happened. As I came out of the daze I was in, I could only see a wall of snow in front of me. The front end of my cab was buried up to the windshield.

"Damn! Here we go again," I muttered. "Hey, Dave! Oh, Dave?!"

"Yeah, John."

"I'm stuck at Price Stopper."

"What happened now, 'Snow Bank'?" Let me guess, you're stuck in a snow bank."

"Well, not really," I humbly replied. "I'm just embedded, up to my windshield, in this huge mountain of snow, and I can't get out."

"Borrow yourself a shovel and dig yourself out," Dave replied with a chuckle.

"Yeah right," I responded in a dejected tone.

"I'll be right down to help you, so sit tight."

At this point Rob and Mike walked over to me to see if they could help me out.

John "the Milkman" Wallin

"Can we give you a hand?" Mike offered. Then he and Rob started clapping.

"Everybody out here is a wise guy."

"Do you want me to go back to the store and get a shovel for you?" Rob chuckled.

"I'm going to need a lot more then a shovel to get this beast out of here. Dave's coming up to help me, and he probably has a chain. I'll get Dave to get another cab out here for you guys. By the way you guys don't have to pay me for this, but if you want you can tip me," I said with a smirk. They just laughed and headed back to the store to wait for another cab.

Scenes In The Rearview Mirror

John "the Milkman" Wallin

Date: March 28, 1998
Time: 5:40 pm
Holiday/Event: ---
Occurrence: Snow Pile

One day when I awoke in the late afternoon, I looked out my window and noticed that the sun was shining. Of course, for the most part, the sun doesn't shine in Cortland until around July.

"Hmm," I said to myself, "It seems like a nice day. Looks like ninety-percent of the snow has melted. There's no way I could get stuck in a snow bank. Nah—screw it. I'm not going to go in to work. With my luck, some crazy thing will happen."

I quickly went back to bed and had a dream of a beautiful and favorite customer of mine, Liz. Suddenly someone's car alarm went off outside of my apartment building, waking me from my beautiful dream.

"Hmm," I pondered. "Maybe I will go in to work tonight after all. Maybe I'll get lucky and run into Liz somewhere."

So I got myself ready, got a bite to eat and went in to work.

When I arrived, unusually on time, the Chevy Caprice party wagon that I usually drove was waiting for me. I

Scenes In The Rearview Mirror

anxiously hopped in, with one thing in mind of course, and radioed, "Hey Dave, I'm in and raring to go."

"I can't believe it!" Dave exclaimed. "You're on time for once."

"Well you know, it's such a nice day and everything."

"He probably can't wait to pick up his honey at Clark Hall," Little Indian wisecracked.

I said to myself, 'Boy, he knows me better than I thought.'

"Go get the St. Charles Hotel," Dave ordered. "There's a couple that needs a ride to the Cortland Diner."

"I'm after it."

Right before I pulled up in front of the St. Charles Hotel, I could see a pile of snow about ten feet long by eight feet wide and about six inches deep. I figured there was no way I could get stuck in such a small pile of snow like this, so I pulled up in front over the pile of snow. I waited the usual five minutes and nobody came out.

"This is fifteen;" I radioed to Dave, "there's nobody coming out, so I'm going to take off."

"Okey dokey, we have a time call at 6:00 pm to pick up Jesse the manager, at Mark's Pizzeria. It's 5:50 pm now, so you might as well head on over."

"I'm after it."

197

John "the Milkman" Wallin

I started to take off from the St. Charles and to my amazement—unlike everyone else's—I sure enough got stuck in the pile of snow.

"Hey Butch," I radioed to one of the other cabbies.

"Yeah, John. What's up?"

"Can you come over to the St. Charles Hotel for a minute? I have to ask you something." I didn't want anyone else to know what was going on.

"Sure, John," Butch returned.

"What's the matter John?" Dave stepped in. "Are you in some kind of trouble again?"

"No!" I nervously shot back. "Just mind your own business. I have to ask Butch something real quick."

When Butch pulled up behind me, he could see my back tires spinning as I was trying to get out of the snow pile. The Caprices we used were rear wheel drive, which didn't help things at all.

"OK John," Butch radioed, "just put your cab in neutral and I'll push you out."

"Thanks for letting the cat out of the bag, Butch," I returned.

Dave heard everything. "You've got to be kidding me! The last pile of snow left in Cortland and you manage to get stuck in it. I can't believe it!"

"Knowing him, he will probably get stuck in a snow bank in the middle of August," Little Indian assured.

198

Scenes In The Rearview Mirror

"That's okay you guys. Someday, when I own this company, you're going to be fixing these cars instead of driving them."

"Yeah, yeah, whatever," 'Little Indian' replied.

"There you go John," Butch radioed as he easily pushed me out with his cab.

"Thanks Butch. I owe you a cup of coffee."

"How about us?" Dave radioed.

"The only cup of anything that I'm going to get you is going to be a cup of mud."

John "the Milkman" Wallin

> **Date:** June 31, 1998
> **Time:** 5:20 pm
> **Holiday/Event:** ---
> **Occurrence:** "I Never Promised
>   You a Rose Garden"

When you have to make that old mighty dollar, you'll do it no matter what it takes.

One night, four of the company's taxi-cabs were down and there was only two left to choose from. Since I was late—as usual—I got stuck with the lucky prize. All the other drivers took the good cars.

"I'm in and ready to go Dave," I radioed from the office. Dave was dispatching from his car. "Which car do you want me to take?"

"Well, John, you have your choice," Dave replied. "You can either take the red Caprice which has no transmission at all, or you can take the blue Caprice which has no reverse." You could tell Dave was enjoying the situation.

"Well, lets see, that's a difficult decision," I sarcastically replied. "Uh, I'll take the…ummm…let me see. I'll take the Caprice with no reverse."

"Just don't park any place where you can't back out of," Dave chuckled.

Scenes In The Rearview Mirror

"I'll try to remember that." I hopped into my car and started the engine. "Hey Dave, I'm ready to go, but there is just one problem."

"What's that?"

"My cab is parked facing the building and I can't back out."

"All right; just hang loose. I'll be right down to help you push it out."

"This is going to be a lot of fun tonight," I mumbled to myself.

"Dave, where are you?" I asked, after fifteen minutes elapsed.

"I'm turning into the parking lot right now," Dave replied.

"Oh yeah, I see ya."

Dave then pulled up along side of me and stepped out of his cab.

"Now Dave, I know you're getting old and everything, but are you sure you're not going to hurt yourself?"

"Hey, I may be getting older, but I can still run circles around you."

"Yeah, yeah, all right," I humored him. "I have the car in neutral. On the count of three, push," I commanded as we both stood in front.

"Push harder," Dave strained. "Boy this car is heavier than I thought."

"OK, one more time! On three—push! Push it out towards the middle of the parking lot," I directed as we started gaining momentum.

"Phew. We did it," Dave commended. "The bones just aren't what they use to be."

"Bones?! I would think that all that bone has turned to cartilage by now," I busted.

"Just shut up and go get Nubig Hall. There's a bunch of students that want to go to Wally World."

"I'm after it."

Five minutes later I pulled up to front of Nubig Dining Hall and six college students hopped into my cab.

"I have Nubig Dining Hall, Dave, and we are going to Wally World," I radioed. I then turned to the college students and asked, "How are you guys doing?

"We're doing pretty well," one of the girls in the back replied.

"Let's see, I'll go into the loading dock here to turn around. Whoops! Great!"

"What's the matter cabbie?" one of the guys in the back asked.

"I forgot, I have no reverse!"

"Do you want us to get out and push you?" the guy sitting in the front with his girlfriend asked.

"Sure why not," I thankfully replied. "This is fifteen, Dave; I have to step out for a few. I pulled into this

Scenes In The Rearview Mirror

loading dock to turn around, and now we have to push the car out."

"I told you not to forget that you don't have any reverse," Dave scolded.

"Yeah, well you know these cabs are usually equipped with reverse," I yelled back in a snit.

So we all pushed the cab back out into the road and away we went.

Ten minutes later I dropped the students off at Wally World and radioed to Dave that I was clear.

"Go get 787 Lime Hollow Road," Dave returned. "And don't pull in the driveway. You won't be able to back out."

"Okey Dokey, Kemosabee. I'll try to remember."

Ten minutes later, as I approached 787 Lime Hollow Road, this huge deer jumped out in front of me. "Phew, that was close," I said to myself after I swerved to miss it.

As I regained my composure I noticed that I had passed number 787. I then decided to do a three-point turn in front of this white house with a huge flower garden in front. I would have pulled in front of the driveway, but it was filled with a bunch of cars.

"Damn!" I yelled. I forgot—once again—that I had no reverse. I saw this huge eighteen-wheeler heading towards me, so I slammed the car into drive and drove

203

John "the Milkman" Wallin

up over the huge garden to avoid being hit by the truck. "That was close! I'd better get the hell out of here!" I started to panic.

I pulled a u-turn, destroying the rest of the flower bed, and headed down the road. By this time, the guy I was supposed to pick up a few houses away was waiting for me in front of his house.

"Hop in," I yelled as I pulled to him.

"It sounds like you're in a rush," the gentleman said. He didn't see me run over the flowerbed a few houses away.

"Yeah, well we're kind of busy," I nervously replied. My conscious was really starting to bother me for running through that poor guy's flowerbed.

A few miles down the road, as I made my turn onto Route 13, a sheriff spotted me and pulled me over.

"Good evening, officer," I humbly stated. I was trying to cover up, but the guilt was written all over my face. My customer still didn't know what was going on.

"Can I see your license please?" the officer politely replied. "Do you know why I pulled you over?"

"Uh, no," I innocently returned.

"We received a report a few minutes ago that someone drove through this guy's flowerbed on Lime Hollow Road."

Scenes In The Rearview Mirror

"Really? Hmm, I wonder who could have done such a thing."

"Well, by the looks of it, it was probably you. Please step out of the car."

"I'm in deep shit now," I mumbled to myself.

"Where do you think all of these pretty flowers came from?" the officer asked as he pointed to my bumper and grille. I could hear my passenger starting to laugh as he caught on.

"Uh, I'm getting my car ready for the Tournament of Roses Parade?"

"I don't think so," the officer replied. By this time my passenger was in stitches. "I'm going to have to write you out a ticket, for something. I don't know what, but I'll figure it out. You're also going to have to pay for that guy's flowerbed. I'll be right back." The officer walked back to his patrol car shaking his head.

"Oh, shut up!" I yelled to my customer in the back seat, who was still laughing. "Hey Dave, are you out there?"

"Yeah John, go ahead."

"Listen, I'm not feeling very well, so I'm going to drop my passenger off and then head on home."

"Yeah, I know its really tough riding with no reverse. OK, John. I'll see you later," Dave returned, as he thought that was the only reason.

205

John "the Milkman" Wallin

My customer started laughing again, and I exclaimed, "If this leaks out and anyone finds out, I'm going to wring your neck!"

Scenes In The Rearview Mirror

Date: **August 9, 1998**
Time: **7:16 pm**
Holiday/Event: ----
Occurrence: **Snow Cone**

"Where are you sitting, John?" Dave radioed.

"I'm at the Youth Bureau trying to get younger," I returned. The Youth Bureau is a place in the City of Cortland where all the teenagers hang out, socialize, play games and watch bands. Many of the cab drivers would meet there to window chat, since the parking lot was so large. "Why? What's up?"

"Nothing," Dave came back. "I'm just wondering."

"I think I'm going to go over to the convenience store and get a soda pop, pop."

"Take your time. There's nothing going on, son."

Ten minutes later, I was back in my cab.

"Dave."

"Yeah, John?"

"You're not going to believe this, but I'm stuck."

"Where are you?"

"I'm on Port Watson Street, stuck in a snow bank."

"Yeah, right," Dave chuckled. "Knowing you, I wouldn't be surprised if you got stuck in a snow bank in August."

207

John "the Milkman" Wallin

"Seriously, though, I'm heading back over to the Youth Bureau. By the way, where's Little Indian?"

"He stopped home for dinner," Dave impatiently replied. "Now leave me alone. I want to take a snooze." Dave was parked somewhere in one of his cool, shady hiding spots. He didn't like to fraternize or get into company politics with the other cab drivers.

"Sheesh!" I groused. "What a grouch!"

I pulled into the huge Youth Bureau's lot and headed for the back. Before I could get myself situated, Dave informed me there was a time call waiting at Wickwire Pool. I pulled a u-turn and proceeded back towards the parking lot exit.

The Bureau's parking lot sat at a slant, making half of the lot significantly lower than the other half. In the middle of the lot sat an orange traffic barrel, marking the site of a caved in storm drain. It also had a bunch of orange traffic cones around it. I was driving a 1988, midnight blue, Caprice station wagon which we called the paddy wagon. It made a professional football tackler look small in it. The driver, who used the car before me, weighed around four hundred pounds. After a while, the driver's seat became beveled out and made me look even shorter yet. I could hardly see over the steering wheel.

Suddenly, I crashed head on into the orange barrel and surrounding traffic cones. I started to panic. I thought

208

Scenes In The Rearview Mirror

that if I sped up a bit, maybe the barrel and all the traffic cones that were stuck underneath my cab would become dislodged. No such luck.

I finally stopped the car and a couple of teenagers, who of course found my predicament amusing, came over and pulled all the traffic cones and orange barrel loose.

A moment later, as I was inspecting my car to make sure there wasn't any damage done, two cop cars pulled into the parking lot. I realized that some "responsible" adult inside the Bureau, must have called them.

"Hey Dave, are you awake?" I radioed, in a tone that sounded like a kid that was in trouble.

"Yeah, kind of," Dave replied. "What's up?"

"Well, you're not going to believe this, but I ran over a bunch of traffic cones at the Youth Bureau, and the cops are here making up an accident report."

"Did you do any damage to the cab?" Dave wanted to know.

"No," I replied, "not that I can see."

"Then why did you wake me up?"

Just then, two more police cruisers entered the parking lot. "Either there's a sale on doughnuts at the Youth Bureau snack bar," I mumbled to myself, "or business must be really slow."

"Hey, Dave."

"Yeah, John?"

209

John "the Milkman" Wallin

"You're not going to believe this," I continued.

"Try me."

"There are now four cop cars, and one of Cortland's finest is taking pictures."

"What happened, John?" "Little Indian" radioed. He had just come back from dinner. "Did you mug someone?"

"No," Dave responded. "He ran over a snow cone."

"You've got to be kidding!" Little Indian yelled. "Nice going, 'Snow Cone'!"

"Yeah, and he was just starting to lose the 'Snow Bank' nickname," Dave noted.

"You guys want to keep your comments to yourself," I impatiently cut in. "I have a situation here!"

Dave chuckled. "Yeah, he might get three to six in the state penitentiary for cone-icide!"

Little Indian couldn't stop laughing.

"I can't believe this! These cops have nothing better to do than make an accident report over some ridiculous snow cone?!" I blurted. "If the city had fixed the damn sinkhole two months ago like they should have, this wouldn't have happened!"

"Yeah, you probably would have hit the building instead!" Dave wisecracked.

"Very funny," I replied, to the sound of his and Little Indian's laughter.

210

Singing Cabbie

I used to try to break the ice and tension between myself and my customers when there

was dead silence between us, or if they were very uptight about something or other. When a situation or conflict would arise between my customers, I would try to break the tension by singing, or sometimes, when appropriate, by cracking a joke or two to get their minds off the situation at hand. Other times I would sing to myself just because I love to sing.

One day I picked up a little old lady in Homer who was going to Cortland to visit her

daughter. When she hopped into my cab, she sternly told me to "step on it." I wanted to say "step on what?" But I didn't. She might have kicked my butt. Anyway, I was in a pretty good mood so I began singing--very low--one of my favorite tunes "Your Smilin' Face" by James Taylor.

John "the Milkman" Wallin

"Whenever I see your smiling face,
I have to smile myself
'Cuz I love you,
yes I do
Whenever you give me that pretty little pout,
it turns me inside out
There's something about you babe,
I don't know…"

She then interrupted and exclaimed, "If you're going to sing it, sing it out loud!" So I did.

"Maybe it's amazing a man like me can feel this way
Tell me how much longer
it can grow stronger every day…"

Shortly after I finished the song, we arrived at her daughter's place in Cortland. I asked her if I pared for the audition. She said yes, and paid for the fare with a five dollar tip, to boot. I thought to myself, 'Man I ought to sing to these customers more often.' So from then on I did, and my nickname, "the Singing Cabbie," was given to me. Here, I present to you some of my favorite, finely *tuned,* 'Singing Cabbie' stories.

Scenes In The Rearview Mirror

Date: February 20, 1999
Time: 10:00 pm
Holiday/Event: Grand Funk Railroad Cover
Band Concert
Occurrence: 4 Parti, for Patti

It was a usual busy Saturday night, and I was given a call to pick up 4 Parti Drive. I was hoping that my charge would be the pretty young woman I had picked up many times before. When I arrived at her house a few minutes later, my hunch proved correct. It was Patti.

"Hi Patti," I yelled out my window as she walked down the sidewalk towards my cab. "How the heck are ya?"

"I'm OK, how are you?"

"Pretty good. Where are you going this evening?"

"Take me to the Third Rail. The cover band for Grand Funk Railroad is playing tonight." The Third Rail was a bar on the south end of the city, and was named such because the building had been a railroad station many years before.

"I have 4 Parti Drive and we're going to the Third Rail," I radioed to Dave Churchill (D.C.) who was dispatching from his car.

John "the Milkman" Wallin

"So you're going to drive Patti to a party from Parti Drive, eh?" D.C. replied in his punny way. "Take good care of her." D.C. had Patti in his cab many times as well.

"So, how has life been treating you lately, Patti?" I asked.

"Pretty good. I have no complaints."

A few moments later we pulled up in front of the Third Rail, and Patti paid the fare. She then walked around the front of the cab, leaned into my open window and asked if I could pick her up at 1:00 am I could smell the musk she was wearing, and hardly could refuse anything she would have requested of me. I told her that I would definitely see her later.

"Did you drop Patti off?" D.C. radioed as I pulled away.

"Yep, I sure did," I replied, feeling totally rejuvenated from her beauty and the smell of her musk.

"Sounds like you're sweet on her," D.C. commented with his usual friendly sore throat-like voice.

"Yeah, well, you know," I returned, not wanting to go into detail.

"Yeah, I know," D.C. returned with a giggle. "I'll write that down on the log to remind you when it's time to pick her up.

Scenes In The Rearview Mirror

"You don't need to do that. I won't be able to get her out of my head."

"Yeah, yeah, just behave when you do get her, ya hear?"

"You know me, D.C."

"Yeah, that's the trouble," D.C. concluded, "I know you too well."

John "the Milkman" Wallin

Date: **February 21, 1999**
Time: **12:55 am**
Holiday/Event: **---**
Occurrence: **"I'm In Love With A Girl**
That I'm Talking About"

"Hey, John," D.C. radioed.

"Yeah, what do you want?"

"You didn't forget Patti, did ya?"

"No, I'm on my way, "Tharteen"," I sarcastically replied, because D.C.'s cab was number 13 and being from the Deep South, he pronounced it that way. I did a pretty good impersonation of D.C. In fact, one time when Dave Thompson (D.T.) was dispatching, I radioed to him using D.C.'s number, and mimicking D.C.'s voice. I announced that "he" was stepping out for five minutes. Since D.C. never called to D.T. that he was back in, he didn't get a call for four-five minutes. I never heard the end of that.

When I arrived at the bar, I could see the bouncer, Tom Fisk, standing by the exit of the bar. He was talking with a man that had "lead singer" written all over him. The band was between sets.

Tom was a friend of mine from many years before. He and his best friend Ron Hess and I would meet at a mutual

Scenes In The Rearview Mirror

friend's house and party all the time. Our mutual friend owned a house on Monroe Heights where we listened to CD's, played chess, smoked a bong and watched the pretty college girls outside his picture window. I nicknamed Tom and Ron, Cheech and Chong because Tom partied just as hard as Cheech, and Ron laughed like Chong.

"Hey, Tom," I yelled across the parking lot.

"What do you want?" he replied in his usual impatient tone.

"Come over here. I want to talk to you."

"Well, make it fast," he snapped as he approached my cab. What do you want?"

"Do you think you could get the lead singer of the band over here? I want to talk to him."

"What makes you think he's the lead singer?" Tom asked.

"I'm very good at telling what people do for a living," I patiently replied. I can tell what *you* do for a living, besides being a bouncer."

"What's that?" Tom curiously asked.

"You're a garbage man."

"Very funny," Tom replied.

"Just go get the dude, will ya?" I was starting to get impatient myself. "I'll give you a free ride later when you go home." Tom used my cab company to go to and from work.

217

John "the Milkman" Wallin

"OK," Tom answered, having no problem sealing the deal. He went over to the lead singer of the band and asked him to come over to me.

"What can I do for you?" the lead singer asked, as he approached my cab.

"Are you the lead singer of the band?" I asked.

"You've got that right." he confidently replied.

"I thought I saw that in you. You look the part."

"What can I do for you?"

"Well, I was wondering if I could audition for your band," I replied. I wasn't taking the whole thing too seriously. "I'd like to pursue my singing career that just started this morning."

"This morning? Hmm," he replied in a confusing tone of voice.

"Yeah, this morning when I woke up from a dream where I was a lead singer in a rock 'n' roll band," I joked.

"Oh, so you want to take my job?" he countered.

"Not really. I thought that maybe you could just critique me and see if I have any potential."

"Why not? Give it a go. I've got some time before we do the last set."

At the same time, Patti approached my cab with a suspicious look on her face, and quietly hopped in the back seat. I started to break into one of Grand Funk's

218

Scenes In The Rearview Mirror

(Railroad's) staples. I tried to direct my singing to both of them--for different reasons, of course.

> *"I'm in love with a girl*
> *that I'm talking about*
> *I'm in love with a girl*
> *that I can't live without*
> *I'm in love, but*
> *I sure picked a bad time,*
> *to be in love.*
> *A bad time to be in love..."*

"That's great!" the singer exclaimed.

"So do I get your job?" I asked, breaking into a smile.

"Sure! You can sing a song with Mack Sams next time we come to Cortland to play."

"That's way too cool!" I earnestly replied. "But who is this "Sams" character?"

"He's one of our roadees who just finished singing 'Locomotion' with us." "Locomotion" was one of Grand Funk Railroad's more famous hits from the 70's when they changed their name to Grand Funk.

"OK!" I was starting to get serious about the whole thing. "So I'll see you the next time you play in Cortland, but I have one question to ask you."

John "the Milkman" Wallin

"Sure, shoot," the lead singer replied.

"Is it just a coincidence that the Grand Funk *Railroad* cover band is playing at an old train station building called The Third Rail, or did you plan it that way?"

"Well, it sort of happened on its own, but when we heard the name of the venue, we had to pull the trigger on it." He paused, sliding his mirrored sunglasses down the bridge of his nose to look me in the eye. "Did that answer your question?"

"Good enough," I replied, with a tone of respect that the lead singer definitely earned. "Hey, thanks for your time. I've gotta take Patti, here in the back, back home."

"Good night. I'll see you the next time we come to Cortland to play."

After I took off, I looked at the dude in my rearview mirror and saw him slowly ambling in his boots as he disappeared into the bar.

When I dropped Patti off a few minutes later, I asked her if she liked my singing and if she would be interested in going out to dinner with me. She said that she liked my singing, but that she had a boyfriend. I may not have gotten the main prize, but at least I got a future gig with the band.

Scenes In The Rearview Mirror

Date: 1998 to 2000
Time: Every Saturday Night
Holiday/Event: ---
Occurrence: Ray, Kelley,
Amadu and the Crew

It all started out one weekend when I first picked the crew up at the Dark Horse, a college bar on Main Street. They were all going to Randall Hall on campus. As soon as they hopped in my cab, the Billy Joel song "It's Still Rock 'N' Roll To Me" came on the classic rock station that I was listening to. We all sang to the song at the top of our lungs, and the last note came as I pulled up in front of Randall Hall five minutes later. The next weekend when they called my cab company, they requested me. This time they were going to Woodman's Pub on Main Street.

"Hi, John," Kelley yelled as the crew hopped in my cab, "how are ya?"

"I'm OK, I guess. It's been a long night already, and I still have six hours to go."

"Why don't you just park your cab and come in with us for a few drinks?" Ray offered.

"I would, but I really need the money and we're starting to get busy out here," I replied.

221

John "the Milkman" Wallin

"Maybe some other time," Amadu followed up. "Hey, put on WSUC-FM, oldies radio. Maybe there's a Billy Joel song playing on that station." They loved Billy Joel just as much as I did, since we all grew up in the same area on Long Island that he did.

"I would, but my boss hasn't replaced this lousy stereo yet and it's starting to cut in and out." Ray took notice of the 10" x 3" gash in the dash from my pounding on it every time I wanted to get it to play.

"Why don't you sing us a song Mr. Taxi Man?" Kelley requested.

"Sure, why not." So I start singing Billy Joel's signature song, "Piano Man."

"It's nine o'clock on a Saturday,
the regular crowd shuffles in
There's an old man sitting next to me,
making love to his tonic and gin
He said, son can you play me a memory?
I'm not really sure how it goes,
but it's sad and it's sweet,
and I knew it complete,
when I wore a younger man's clothes
da-da-da, di-da-da-da, da-da-di-da-da, da-dum
Sing us a song, you're the piano man, sing us a song tonight

Scenes In The Rearview Mirror

Well we're all in the mood for a melody and you've got us feeling all right

"That's awesome, Johnny!" Kelley exclaimed. Kelley called me Johnny, as I was called when I was a child by my cousins. She was so cool.

"Sing another one," Ray requested.

"Maybe when I pick you up after the bars close."

"OK, Cabbie Man," Amadu said as I pulled up in front of Woodman's Pub. Ray paid the fare, as always, and gave me the usual five dollar tip.

Now I've never met Billy Joel personally, but I've met a lot of people who did when I lived on Long Island. I used to frequent a nightclub in Roslyn, where Billy played at times with his band before he became famous. Whenever Billy showed up to party with his friends in the days after he became the "Piano Man," the manager would lock the doors and Billy would unexpectedly play some of his famous tunes to everyone's delight. I never was at the nightclub for any of those occasions, but I saw him in concert a couple of times.

One night while I was shopping in a grocery store in Ithaca in upstate New York, I was telling the check out girl that I drove a cab for a living, and to make my job more interesting, I would intro a song on the radio with one of my D.J. deliveries. I told her that I would get

223

John "the Milkman" Wallin

everybody to sing the song. Then I started to tell her about times when some of my favorite customers and I would sing Billy Joel songs, and a gentleman standing behind me overheard the conversation. After we both made our purchases and headed for the door, he told me that he drove a cab in Ithaca and graduated with Billy Joel in Hicksville, Long Island. Small world.

Scenes In The Rearview Mirror

Date: **August 7, 2001**
Time: **7:18 pm**
Holiday/Event: ---
Occurrence: **I Wish It Would Rain On Me**

One early evening in the beginning of August, I was sitting at the local convenience store parking lot across from the clock tower. I was waiting for a call to come in. In the ghost town-like city of Cortland, it was extremely hot and muggy. Approximately seventy percent of the residents were away on vacation. The students were still on *theirs*.

I couldn't turn my car off because there was a good chance it would not have started again. The starter was on its last leg and the owner of my cab company didn't believe in preventive maintenance. He usually waited until the part of the car was totally nonfunctional.

Since I was a part-timer, I always got stuck with the worst running car. My cab smoked very badly, since the oil was never changed. So bad, that the other drivers wouldn't park next to me to window-chat. The black coal-like colored smoke that emanated from my exhaust pipe totally enveloped my cab. The plume of smoke clouded around my cab, much like the one around the Pig Pen character in the *Peanuts* comic strip.

225

John "the Milkman" Wallin

I noticed a city patrol car pulling into the parking lot. He pulled along side my cab.

"You're smoking like a bandit," the officer yelled through his opened car window.

"No, I never saw *Smokey and the Bandit,*" I yelled back. I knew what he really said. I was just trying to be difficult.

"Look at that cloud of smoke around you!"

"What's that? I can't hear you. There's too much smoke in here."

"Turn your damn car off!" the officer demanded.

"What's that?"

"TURN YOUR DAMN CAR OFF!"

"Oh, OK," I yelled back. So I turned my damn car off, and I had to wait a few minutes for the smoke to clear before I could clearly see the officer.

"You know it's illegal to drive that smoke bomb around, don't you?" the officer stated, when the smoke cleared.

"Yeah well, this is the car they gave me, and I have to pay the bills, you know."

"You are going to have to take that thing off the road, or I'm going to ticket you."

My attitude went from wisecracker to serious. "Can't I just stay out here for a couple of more hours until one of the other drivers goes home?" Some of the other drivers went

226

Scenes In The Rearview Mirror

home early during the summer months when business was slow. "This way I'll be able to get another cab.""Well, I don't know."

"Please, officer?"

"I guess. Just for a couple of hours. If I see you after that, I'm going to ticket you and have the car impounded."

"Thanks officer. Anytime you need a ride for you or your family, give me a call, OK?"

"No problem. Don't forget; two hours!"

The officer took off and Dave's voice boomed over the radio, "Car fifteen; where are you?!"

"I'm at the convenience store parking lot across from the clock tower."

"We had a call for Jimmy D. and Amy the bartender to be picked up at the Pine Grove Inn. I was going to give it to you, but you didn't answer when I called you." A few minutes elapsed and Dave commented, "Boy it is a real scorcher out here. It is so hot; I can barely touch the steering wheel."

"Yeah, tell me about it. Earlier I had left a video tape on the dashboard of my personal car and it totally melted. I hope the video rental place won't charge me for their tape being warped."

"It is more like an "act of God" out of your control, you know," Dave added.

John "the Milkman" Wallin

"You know what kind of "act of God" I'd like to happen?"

"What's that?"

"For it to rain."

"Same here. John, I'm going to head out for a time call to pick up Trish and little Kimmy at the Daily Grind."

"OK, Dave."

Little Kimmy and her mother Trish were two of my favorite customers. Kimmy, who was three and a half years old at the time, looked like a little Eskimo. She had jet black hair with bangs down to her eyebrows and wore a white winter ski suit with a pink scarf.

I looked into the sky, and there were some dark storm clouds in the distance. I decided to cruise over to the Youth Bureau where my fellow cabbie, Wingnut, was sitting. When I pulled up alongside him, I put my car into park and it started smoking like a bastard again. The plume of smoke went at least a hundred feet into the sky.

"Turn that damn thing off!" Wingnut yelled.

"Sorry about that," I returned. When the smoke cleared a few minutes later, I commented, "I can't believe how hot and muggy it is out here. I can't wait until the days start getting cooler again."

"The summer is far from over," Wingnut assured me.

Scenes In The Rearview Mirror

I continued my whining. "I can't believe I haven't had a call in two hours."

"Yeah, you know how it is," Wingnut explained, "the month of August is always the slowest time of the year. The students will be back in a couple of weeks or so, and then things will start to pick up."

"That's true."

Just then I heard the Who song, "Love, Reign O'er Me," come over the classic rock station I was listening to. I cranked up the volume and started singing, "Rain on me, rain o'er me."

Wingnut was looking at me as though I was nuts. As the song gained more momentum towards the middle, I cranked it up even louder and started screaming, "Hold me, hold me." Wingnut started to laugh.

"And they call me Wingnut!" Wingnut exclaimed. By this time, I could see some kids in front of the Youth Bureau taking notice of my singing. I thought maybe it was my time to shine, to let my hair down and be in the rock 'n' roll spotlight.

I started singing even louder. "Love, reign o'er me, rain on me, rain on me…" Wingnut was in stitches at that point.

"You'd better calm down," Wingnut warned. "I can see the veins in your neck starting to pop out, and your face is starting to turn red. You are going to have a stroke…Uh oh!"

I looked over in the direction Wingnut was staring, and I could see a police officer walking towards us. As the climax of the song was coming, I stepped up the vocals even louder than before. "Love, rain on me, rain on me, rain on me. Hold me, hold me. Luuuove!"

Wingnut could hardly contain himself as the police officer reached us. "Is there a problem here?" the officer asked. Wingnut was in tears.

"Not really officer," I replied." I'm just relieving a little stress."

"The whole freakin' neighborhood can hear you," the officer speculated. The kids were applauding my performance just as the first few drops of rain began to fall. The storm winds began to blow, and the leaves of the neighboring trees began to show their whiter backs.

"Encore! Encore!" a couple of the kids yelled.

Under his breath, Wingnut mumbled, "You prayed for rain, John."

"I'm sorry officer, but I really love rock n' roll. I couldn't help it," I said, trying to keep a straight face.

"Just keep it down!" the officer demanded. And what are you laughing at?" He directed his attention towards Wingnut. After a moment of awkward silence, the cop walked back to his car and drove off. As everything was

Scenes In The Rearview Mirror

back to normal, Wingnut and I went about our usual conversation while enjoying the cooler temperatures the rain had brought.

John "the Milkman" Wallin

Date: **April 3, 2002**
Time: **1:10 am**
Holiday/Event: ---
Occurrence: **Free Stylin'**

I was given a call to pick up 18 Maple Avenue where there was a mixture of college houses and privately owned homes. When I made my turn onto Maple, I tuned my stereo to the local country station, and Shania Twain's "I Feel Like a Woman" was playing. A few minutes

later as I approached the young woman's house, I started to sing at the top of my lungs… "I feel like a woman." I passed her home by three houses as she stood in bewilderment. As I looked into the rearview mirror, I could see her shaking her head. I jammed on my brakes, put the car in reverse and backed up to her.

"Are you into woman's lib?" she asked with a smirk on her face as she hopped into my cab.

"Sorry about that," I replied. "I got carried away. I really like Shania Twain."

"Yeah, I think she's pretty awesome myself."

"Where are you going?"

"I'm going to the Armadillo Bar on Main Street."

"I have 18 Maple, and we're going to the Armadillo," I radioed to my dipspatcher, Dave.

232

Scenes In The Rearview Mirror

"All right, Milkman," Dave returned. "When you're clear, pick up Escapes. There are some dudes who need to go to Higgins Hall."

I thought to myself, "Milkman?" Dave rarely calls me John, let alone "Milkman.'" I then radioed, "Are you all right, Dave?"

"Yeah, I'm just fine, John. I had a tooth pulled earlier and I feel just fine."

"You feel fine?"

"Yeah, a few of those pills and I'm raring to go."

"Oh, I get it." I thought I would have a little fun with Dave, while the opportunity arose.

"Hey, Dave, you should take those pills more often."

"Why is that, John?"

"Because I like it when you're nice, and not your miserable, cranky self."

"You're such a sweet person," Dave responded, in a humble and dreamy tone of voice.

"Well, I guess I'm not going to be able to piss Dave off tonight," I mumbled to myself. I figured I'd give it one more shot.

"Hey Dave, you can get Escapes yourself. I'm going home to have a couple of beers after I clear the Armadillo, you old fogie! Have a nice night, you bonehead."

233

John "the Milkman" Wallin

"You too, Milkman. I'll see you tomorrow. Drink a beer for me."

"Yeah, whatever," I replied with an "I give up" tone in my voice. "After I clear at the Armadillo, I'll get Escapes Night Club."

So I dropped the young woman off and headed down the strip towards Escapes. When I pulled up, there were three college students that were dressed to the hilt in their Tommy Hilfiger apparel.

"Hop in, dudes," I yelled through the passenger side window that I opened from the control buttons on my armrest. "Where are you going?"

"To Higgins Hall," replied the more aggressive of the three, who hopped in the front seat.

"I have three smooth customers, Dave, and we're going to Higgins Hall." A few seconds elapsed and I didn't hear any response. "Oh, Dave? Hey, Dave... I guess he's parked somewhere, and he's out for the count."

"What do you mean?" asked the most aggressive and more sleek of the three.

"My dispatcher took some pain killers to relieve the pain from a tooth that he had pulled."

"Wow, that must be some pretty potent stuff he's on," one of the dudes sitting in the back seat noted.

"What's your name, cabbie?" the dude sitting in front asked.

234

Scenes In The Rearview Mirror

"John, but you can call me Milkman, if you want. What's yours?"

"I'm Tarik, the Sleek Sheik, and those are my two homies in the back, Kariev and J-Rod."

"Nice to meet you guys."

"Can you turn the radio to 107.9?" J-Rod asked. 107.9 was the local rap station out of Syracuse.

"Sure, no problem."

The "Rappers Three" were quietly rapping to a top forty rap song when my stereo crapped out for the zillionth time. With all the dead silence, I decided to break into a rap of my own.

" *We're heading in my taxi, over the college hill*
Underneath the starry skies, the whole world's lying still
Except for the "Rappers Three" and I
We're really flyin' high
We're the center of the universe
And we're all rappin' free style…"

I guess I really impressed them because when I finished free stylin' they all slapped each other high five and patted me on the back.

When I dropped them off at Higgins Hall, they paid the fare and gave me a five dollar tip.

This Is Car 15; I'm Steppin' Out Momentarily…

There were many nights, especially during the coldest days of winter, when I would get only one or two chances in twelve hours to step out for a quick cup of coffee. There were also many nights that I would step out for longer periods, especially during the summer months. After all, man does not live by work alone.

My friend and *dip*spatcher, Dave, wasn't too appreciative of the times that I stepped out for more than five minutes, but with his easy-going disposition, he always seemed to get over it.

Here are some of the many times that I stepped out on my friend Dave and left him hanging. I can only say that my feelings of guilt were overridden by all of the great times I had.

Scenes In The Rearview Mirror

Date: September 1, 1999
Time: 11:21 pm
Holiday/Event: ---
Occurrence: **Tickle Our Ivories**

It was the night of my birthday and I had to work since two of the full time drivers had just quit. I didn't really mind too much because I had partied with some friends the night before. I was given a call to pick up the Plaza Movie Theater on Tompkins Street, right outside of the city. Seven college girls were waiting outside the theater as I pulled up.

"Where are you going?" I asked as the girls stepped into my taxi. Three of them hopped into the front and four hopped into the back.

"To Nu Sigma Chi on Prospect Terrace," the one sitting in the front seat replied.

"Isn't that a sorority house?" I asked.

"Yep," the girls in the back proudly and simultaneously answered.

It was a real tight fit with the three girls sitting in the front, but I didn't mind that at all. Every time I made a right hand turn, I turned the wheel really hard. That made things even cozier.

John "the Milkman" Wallin

"What time are you working until, Mr. cabbie man?" one of the girls sitting in the back asked.

"Right around 5:00 this morning. That is, if things slow down enough with all the college partying and everything. There have been times when I've been out here until 8:00 in the morning, driving students home from their all night partying."

"What time did you start?" the other girl in the back wanted to know.

"Oh, around six hours ago," I sighed.

"Wow, twelve hours. That must be rough," the girl in the front said.

"You've got that right."

"We're having a party that started around 10:00 pm. Why don't you come in for a beer?" the first girl in the back seat suggested.

"Sure, sounds like a plan." I couldn't resist hanging out with such beautiful college girls.

A few minutes later, we arrived at the sorority house and I radioed to Dave my *dip*spatcher, "I'm clear at Nu Sigma Chi, and I'm stepping out momentarily to get a cup of coffee." I thought to myself that Dave would never know that I was joining the girls for a beer at their sorority house.

"OK, car fifteen. Just make it fast. We are starting to get busy!" Dave commandingly replied.

238

Scenes In The Rearview Mirror

"Yeah, right," I mumbled to myself. My tone of voice matched a kid's, saying, "Whatever."

As we entered the three-story house, the first thing I noticed was a half keg of beer sitting in the entranceway. The entranceway was adjoined to the living room.

"Grab yourself a beer, and make yourself at home Mr. Cabbie Man," one of the girls graciously offered.

"Thanks!" My beer cup was already half full. I then walked into the living room and saw a huge grand piano off to one side. It looked like it dated back to the early 1900's. "Nice piano," I commented. The black paint was almost a brown color in certain parts, giving the piano an antique and rustic look.

"Yeah, that piano has been here for at least forty years or so. It was here twenty-five years ago when my mom went to school here," one of the beautiful sorority girls said. "Do you play, Taxi Man?"

"Yeah, a little bit," I humbly replied.

"Play a song for us -- please?"

"Yeah, play a song for us, Mr. Cabbie Man," another girl yelled.

I could hardly refuse such a willing audience. "Well, all right. You've talked me into it."

Actually, I could only play one song, "Colour My World," by Chicago, so I had to make that a good one. I

239

John "the Milkman" Wallin

cracked my knuckles, trying to show that I knew what I was doing, and began to play.

"As time goes on I realize
just what you mean to me
And now, now that you're near
Promise your love that I've waited to share
and dream of our moments together
Colour my world of loving you..."

By the time I finished the song, about fifteen girls had gathered around the piano. Two of them were even sitting on the piano bench to either side of me. They all applauded and asked me to play another song. I told them maybe in a little bit, and that I needed another beer to loosen up. I thought to myself, 'Phew, I wiggled my way out of this one. I'll have to drink a couple more beers really fast, and then mosey on out of here.' So I drank another four beers and said goodbye to all of the gorgeous sorority girls.

The girls seemed disappointed. "Can't you stay a little longer and play another song for us, Mr. Piano Man?"

"No, I really have to go. It's been half an hour and I need to get back to my cab. Thanks anyway, maybe some other time."

Scenes In The Rearview Mirror

When I got back to my cab, I heard Dave yelling over the radio. "Car fifteen! Where the hell are you?"

I waited a few minutes to collect my thoughts and come up with some excuse as to why I was out for half an hour. "This is fifteen," I finally radioed back to Dave, "I'm back in." I acted as though I had only been out for two minutes.

"Where the heck were you?!" Dave yelled.

"I had a flat tire and my battery went dead." I replied, thinking of all the excuses I could come up with.

"Well, we had to call one of the other drivers in just to cover your butt!" Dave was furious, but I was hardly going to bow down to him.

"Well, I'm here now, so you can send the guy back home," I commanded.

Dave had something else in mind. "No, I think it would be more fitting that you gas it, drag it, and head on home yourself."

After a brief contemplation, I figured that it might work out for the best. "OK, Dave."

So, I gassed it, dragged it, and went on back to the party for a few more beers.

John "the Milkman" Wallin

Date: **July 29, 2000**
Time: **9:45 pm**
Holiday/Event: **Iron Butterfly Concert**
Occurrence: **Free Spirited Butterfly**

It was a warm and humid, late July evening and business was very slow as it usually was at that time of year. The events were plentiful in the small-time city of Cortland. There were fireworks going off to complete the St. Anthony's bazaar and the famous rock band Iron Butterfly was the headliner at Beaudry Park. Beaudry Park is a happening park in Cortland where they have basketball courts, softball and baseball fields and holds many summer events.

My friend Jason Wood told me the day before that he was definitely going to the concert. He asked me if wanted to go with him, but I told him that I had to work.

But, as I said, it was quiet. So quiet that I thought I could probably catch the concert without being missed. There were two local bands playing before Iron Butterfly, and I figured that the main act wouldn't start until around 10:00 pm or so.

"This is car fifteen, I'm stepping out momentarily for a cup of coffee," I radioed.

"Here we go again," Dave my *dip*spatcher mumbled.

242

Scenes In The Rearview Mirror

"What was that?" I barked.

"Nothing, go ahead, do your thing. And make it fast!"

"OK."

So I cruised on over to Beaudry Park, parked my cab and made my way through the park towards the front of the stage. Everyone was drinking their beers and socializing with one another as the stage was being set up for the main act.

As I came closer to the stage, I recognized the back of a guy that turned out, as I expected, to be my buddy Jason. I snuck up to him, making sure that he didn't see me. "Excuse me, sir," I asked from behind, "can I have a sip of your beer?"

He whirled around and grinned at me. "John! What's up? I thought you had to work?"

"Yeah," I said nonchalantly, "but I told them that I was stepping out for a cup of coffee."

"Here, drink the rest of this beer," Jason offered. "I have to go to the bathroom and then I'll get us some more. I'll be right back."

A short time later, Jason came back with two more beers. One was for me, and the other he began to sip on. Iron Butterfly started playing shortly after, and by the time they were done playing their encore song, "Ina Gada Davida," I had finished three beers.

John "the Milkman" Wallin

"What an awesome concert!" Jason exclaimed about an hour later when the band was through playing.

"You can say that again," I replied. "Well, I'd better get back to my cab. They probably – most definitely – have missed me by now."

"OK, John. I'll catch you later."

I quickly made my way through the dense crowd towards the exit of the park. The three beers I had consumed hampered my sense of direction. The fact that I was very tired didn't help either. I went out the wrong exit of the park and had to circumnavigate the entire park before I found the entrance that my cab was parked at.

"This is car fifteen," I called over the radio, trying not to slur my words, "I'm back in."

"You know the routine, car fifteen!" Dave boomed over the radio.

I obviously hadn't gotten away with anything. "Yeah, I know. Gas her, drag her, and head on home," I resignedly replied. "I'll see you tomorrow night, Dave."

"Yeah, whatever," Dave responded with an I-give-up tone in his voice.

I gassed her, dragged her and went home. As soon as I hit the pillow, I fell asleep and dreamed about Liz, a beautiful college girl I had picked up earlier that night.

Scenes In The Rearview Mirror

Date: October 6, 2000
Time: 12:01 am
Holiday/Event: ---
Occurrence: Who's the Hustler Here?

I was dispatched to pick up someone from Dillion's, a local bar on the south end of the city. When I pulled up in front of the bar, I looked through the window and noticed that there were only two people in the place; the bartender and a customer sitting at the bar. When I beeped the horn, I didn't get any response from the bartender or the gentleman. I figured the music was too loud, and they couldn't hear me.

"This is car fifteen, I'm stepping out momentarily to fish this guy out of here," I radioed.

"Okey Dokey," Dave, my *dip*spatcher replied. "Make it fast, though. The bar rush is about to start."

I went into the bar and asked the bartender if anyone called a cab. The gentleman sitting at the bar, who looked to be in his early thirties, with long blond hair, a rock solid build and tattoos on both triceps, told me the guy who called decided to walk. He introduced himself to me as Zach.

"Hey, how would you like to play a game of pool before you take off?" Zach asked.

245

John "the Milkman" Wallin

"Sure," I replied. "Why not? What could it hurt?"

"Can I buy you a drink?" he proffered.

"No, that's all right," I said, declining his offer--an abnormal behavior for me. "I have to drive for another five hours or so."

He handed me three quarters. "Here's seventy-five cents. Go rack 'em and I'll be right back. By the way; you can break."

We played a quick game of eight ball, and I beat him by a couple of balls. "How about another game?" Zach requested. "It won't take long." Zach let me win the first game so he could hustle me and win a lot of money.

I knew what Zach was up to. "All right, why not?" I replied. "Let me go out to my cab and get my coffee. Here's seventy-five cents. Rack 'em and I'll be right back. By the way; you can break."

"Another wise guy," Zach mumbled.

I went out to my taxi-cab and all I heard was Dave screaming over the radio, over and over again, "Are you back in yet, car fifteen?" I grabbed my coffee, shrugged and went back into the bar.

"All right, I'm back. Go ahead and break!" I commanded.

"Hey, before I break, do you want to make things a little more interesting?" Zach the hustler – I mean gentleman – asked.

246

Scenes In The Rearview Mirror

"What did you have in mind?" I asked.

"How about we play straight pool at a dollar a ball?" he suggested, as I could see dollar signs in his eyes.

"Sure, why not? I'm game," I answered, accepting his challenge.

We played for over an hour and a half, and all I can say is that the thickness of the wad of bills that I had in my pocket had tripled.

"Nice playing with you, sir," I respectfully stated, trying to avoid being pulverized by someone who was twice my size. "We should do this again sometime."

Zach obviously was not as pleased with the outcome of our games as I was. "Yeah, yeah, whatever," he responded with a disgusted look on his face.

I bid the bartender a 'fare thee well' and headed for my taxi. "This is car fifteen; I'm back in," I called over the radio. After a couple of minutes with no answer, I tried again. "This is car fifteen, is anybody out there?" There was still no answer. "Hey Dave! Where the heck are you?"

"I'm trying to ignore you," Dave finally replied. "Where have you been? Never mind; I don't want to know."

"Do you want me to gas it and drag it, and head on home?"

John "the Milkman" Wallin

"No," Dave sighed, "not this time. Timmy M. went home early, and I don't exactly relish the thought of being out here alone. Next time you step out for an hour and a half, I'll send you home."

"Thanks, Dave. You the man."

"Yeah, whatever," Dave mumbled, resignedly.

Scenes In The Rearview Mirror

Date: May 9, 2001
Time: 3:11 am
Holiday/Event: ---
Occurrence: What a Drag

I was on my way down Tompkins Avenue to pick up a call at Mark's Pizza on Main Street, when three college dudes flagged me down.

"Where are you guys going?" I yelled out the passenger side window as I came to a quick stop. I was half way to the pizza parlor.

"We're going to Hayes Hall," the more sober of the three answered.

"OK, hop in. I have a call waiting for me at Mark's Pizza, but I'll take you guys home first." Hayes Hall was located a half of a mile back towards the college. They were quite intoxicated and rowdy.

"Thanks, cabbie," the second most sober of the three replied, as they all hopped into the back seat of my cab.

"How are you guys doing?" I asked.

"Cut the rhetoric and just get us home, alright!" the least sober of the three, sitting directly behind me, obnoxiously demanded.

249

John "the Milkman" Wallin

As I looked into the rearview mirror I could see that his shirt was torn at the shoulder, hanging half way down his arm. He had a cut on the bridge of his nose and it appeared that he had been in a fight. He was also slurring his words. I thought to myself, 'I hope this dude doesn't throw up since he is sitting directly behind me.' A moment later, about a block before Hayes Hall, I could hear the dude starting to gag. "I'll let you guys out here," I directed, as I started to slow down.

"Don't worry cabbie, I'll take care of this!" exclaimed the most sober of the three who was sitting in the middle, next to the emesis-ready dude.

He reached over his overly-inebriated friend and opened the door. He took hold of his arm and pushed him half way out of the cab while I was still going twenty miles an hour. The dude's head was only a foot away from the pavement as he began to *toss his cookies* – if you get my flow. I thought to myself, 'I can't believe the nerve one needs to do something like this, and the confidence as well.'

I dropped them off shortly after and headed back to Mark's Pizza.

Scenes In The Rearview Mirror

When I pulled up in front the place, five TC3 students hopped into my cab. I asked them, in an Italian accent, "Where are you a-guys a-going?"

"To the Leaning Tower of *Pizza*," replied the more bold and aggressive student that was sitting in the front.

"Just keep eating your slice of pizza and we'll lean towards taking you to your true destination," I spontaneously replied, returning to my normal accent.

"We are a-going to TC3," the more responsible one of the bunch who was sitting in the back seat said, as the rest were laughing.

"No problem," I replied. So we took off towards the community college in Dryden.

"Hey cabbie; Do you want to get stoned?" the more aggressive one in the front asked.

"I don't do that stuff anymore. It has been five years since the last time I smoked," I nervously replied.

"Come on cabbie, what can it hurt?!" asked one of the other students sitting in the back seat.

"Well...why not. Just a few tokes couldn't hurt." I easily succumbed to their pressure.

John "the Milkman" Wallin

"Here you go cabbie," the aggressive one said as he lit up a joint and passed it over to me.

"Thanks," I replied. So I took a few drags and passed it to the guys in the back seat.

"Hey Mr. Cabbie, can you put some tunes on?" asked the more quiet college student sitting in the back seat.

I gladly obliged. "Here you go, sir." The guy in the front seat passed the joint back to me after the dude sitting in the back passed it back to him. "Take another hit."

I felt like singing that song from the seventies, "Don't Bogart that Joint" ('my friend, pass it over to me'). Instead, I said, "No, I'm fine. I think I've had enough. Remember I still have an hour and a half left on my shift."

Several minutes later I pulled up in front of their dorm and said, "Thanks, guys. That will be thirteen dollars, please."

"Here you go, Mr. Cabbie. There's a two dollar tip in there for you also," the aggressive one in the front seat said.

"Thanks a lot," I replied as I took the money.

Scenes In The Rearview Mirror

He shook my hand with a joint in it, and handed it to me.

"Here is one for the road back to Cortland."

"No thanks; I'm just fine."

So they headed for their dorm, and I took off back to Cortland. I was feeling pretty normal when I first left the TC3 dorms, but then all of a sudden it hit me. I mumbled to myself, "Boy, that was some real potent stuff." I was very tired, and I felt like crawling under a rock. I stopped at the rest stop on the way back, and fell asleep for an hour and a half.

When I woke up--around 5:15 am--the sun was coming up. I collected myself, drove back to Cortland, and radioed, "This is car fifteen; I am back in Cortland. Are you guys busy?"

"No," Dave replied. "Where the hell were you?!"

Dave usually stayed on shift for an extra hour or so to ease the transition from the night shift to the day shift, but I didn't expect him to still be there this late.

"I was so tired that I pulled off at the rest stop here on Rt. 13 and fell asleep."

"Well, couldn't you have told me what you were doing?"

253

"I was too tired to."

"Here we go again!" Dave exclaimed. "Gas her, drag her and go on home."

I felt like saying, 'No s!@#$ Sherlock, my shift ended a half hour ago,' but I didn't want to push my luck. Instead I said, "OK, Dave. I'll see you tomorrow."

When I arrived at the office to do my cash-up, after I gassed and washed my cab, I anxiously anticipated seeing my favorite cabbie.

"Cabbie!" I called, "Cabbie! Where the heck are ya?" I looked under the counter and behind the desk. I couldn't see Cabbie anywhere. I even looked behind the TV – no Cabbie.

"Cabbie – here kitty, kitty."

Cabbie, the company mascot, was a black and white Tabby cat that lived in the office. Every morning when I sat at the counter counting my money, Cabbie would sit there and watch me for as long as it took. It was as though the cat was studying my every move. Cabbie the Tabby was the coolest cat I had ever seen.

"Come here, Cabbie!"

Scenes In The Rearview Mirror

All of the sudden, Cabbie came out of nowhere and leaped up to the counter as I sat down.

After I finished counting my money, I pocketed my commission and tips and deposited my boss's share as well. When I headed towards the door to let Cabbie out, I noticed, through the front door window, the seemingly motionless, spectacular Comet, Hale-Bopp in the early morning sky. What a sight! I thought to myself, 'Now this would be something to get stoned for.'

John "the Milkman" Wallin

Scenes In The Rearview Mirror

Date: May 3, 2001
Time: 12:26 am
Holiday/Event: ---
Occurrence: Party Time

"Hey John."

"Yeah, Dave, wazz-up?"

"Go get the Third Rail. Some girl needs a ride back to Clark Hall."

"I'm after it," I replied. I then mumbled to myself, "Gee, I wonder if it's Liz? She lives at Clark Hall." Liz was one of my favorite customers. She was friendly, beautiful inside and out, and she had the smarts to go with it. She was half Swedish and half Albanian.

A few minutes later, I pulled up in front of the Third Rail and noticed the advertisement on the marquee: The Dave Matthews cover band, Tripping Billies -- Appearing Tonight. "Wow," I mumbled to myself. "I heard that band is awesome." I beeped the horn for my customer. "I wonder how much it costs to get in." I beeped the horn again. "Maybe I can go in to look for my fare and sneak a peek." I beeped once more. "This is car fifteen," I radioed to Dave. "I'm steppin' out momentarily to fish my customer out of here."

"Make it fast," Dave replied in a suspicious tone.

257

John "the Milkman" Wallin

I hopped out of my cab and went into the club. I told the guy at the door that I was just going to go in there to look for my customer, so I didn't have to pay the cover charge. As it turned out, I couldn't find Liz or anyone that called for a cab, so I hung out for ten minutes to check out the Tripping Billies--and I'm glad I did. They were awesome! My buddy Derek, who was one of the bouncers and was on his break, came over to hang out with me and watch the band.

"Hey John, can I buy you a beer?" Derek asked.

"Sure, but only one. I'm driving my cab tonight."

I then thought to myself, 'Hmm, I wonder if Liz is working at Balducci's tonight.' She was a part-time bartender at the popular college bar on Central Avenue. A couple of weeks before, she had asked me to stop by for a drink.

"Here you go, John," Derek said upon his return, offering me a cold draft.

"Thanks, Derek. Any time you need a ride, just give me a call. I'll hook you up," I reciprocated.

"Well, I have to get back to work, John. Nice seeing you."

"All right, dude. I'm going to stop over to Balducci's to see if a friend of mine is working. Thanks for the beer." After I finished my beer, I went back to my cab and headed across town to Balducci's.

258

Scenes In The Rearview Mirror

"Hey Dave, where did John go?" Bulldog radioed.

"He stepped out twenty minutes ago to look for his customer at the Third Rail."

"Sounds like another one of his rendezvous," Bulldog sniffed.

"Yeah ,well, I'm getting pretty tired of it. He'd better get back soon!" Dave barked.

I turned my radio off, so I didn't have to hear their whining and whimpering. When I arrived at Balducci's, I assumed that the place was packed from all the steam that was on the windows. My friend Bennie was carding people at the door.

"Hey Bennie," I called out my window as I pulled up. "Is Liz bartending tonight?"

"Yeah," Bennie answered. "Come on in and hang out for awhile."

"I'll be right in." I parked my cab.

I shook Bennie's hand as I walked into the night club and slowly made my way towards the bar. My earlier estimation turned out to be accurate; the place was totally jam-packed. As I fought my way through the crowd, I could see that Liz was indeed tending bar.

"Hey, Liz!" I yelled, when I finally made it to the bar. "How the heck are ya?"

"Johnny!" she yelled.

John "the Milkman" Wallin

As I got closer to her, I could see the sweat beading on her beautiful cocoa-colored skin. I looked into her Mediterranean Sea-green eyes, and my icy-blue colored eyes started to melt. I thought to myself, 'If this only could be love.' She leaned across the bar and gave me a big fat hug, and I suddenly realized what it meant to seize the moment.

"Can I buy you a beer?" she offered.

"Well," I began.

"Come on, John," Christa cut in. She was my second favorite bartender.

"Why not? Just one, though. I have to drive for a few more hours."

"Yeah, that's what you said last time," Christa laughed.

Just then, one of Christa's many male friends came up to the bar and she gave him a kiss, smack on the lips.

"Hey Christa, what about me?" I half-jokingly asked.

"Sure, come here." I reached over and she kissed me as well. This time, time didn't seem to slow down as much as it had when I hugged Liz.

"You're a taxi-cab driver!" one of the college girls at the bar interjected. "I had you the other night!"

"Believe me," I quipped, "if you had me, I wouldn't have forgotten you." She was gorgeous!

260

Scenes In The Rearview Mirror

"You know what I mean," she innocently stated.

"Yeah, I'm just kidding." I noticed Liz and Christa had climbed onto the bar. I turned to the college girl and asked her what was going on.

"They're getting ready to pour everyone shots of liquor."

I was thinking of saying, 'maybe they'll do a strip tease', but instead I asked, "Standing on the bar?"

"Yeah, they walk up and down the bar, and when all of the patrons open their mouths, which is just about all of them, they pour a few shots down their throats."

Liz then came over to me and said, "Open up, John!"

"No thanks," I replied. "I have to drive the rest of the night."

"Come on, John!" Christa yelled.

"All right," I bowed to the pressure. "Just one shot!"

I opened my mouth and Liz began to pour. I closed my mouth after what felt like two or three shots, but Liz kept on pouring. "You're not supposed to close your mouth, John!" she yelled as the liquor poured all over my face.

"I don't want to get a DWI driving all the drunks home!" I explained, as I cleaned the liquor off my nose and chin.

John "the Milkman" Wallin

"Yeah, that's true," Liz said, agreeing. "Better safe, than sorry."

"I'm gonna take off, Liz. Thanks for the free beer!" I said a few moments later, after Liz and Christa returned to their posts behind the bar.

"I'll probably give you a call later for a ride home when I'm finished here," Liz said in what appeared--to me anyway--to be a sexy tone of voice.

"OK, no problem. I'm at your disposal, 24/7!"

"Thanks, John!" Liz excitedly replied.

"See ya, Christa," I called across the bar.

"See ya, John," Christa replied through a thick wall of noisy chatter. When I got back to my cab a few minutes later, I radioed, "Hey, Dave; I'm back in." Silence was my only answer for several seconds. "Hello? Is anybody out there?" I called again. Still, more silence met my call. I opened my mic and exclaimed, "So I said to myself, self; what does a man have to do to get a response around here?!" I waited for a response, and when none came, I spoke another time into the microphone, "I know you guys are out there…Bulldog; talk to me! Dave?" Finally, I gave up. "All right, I get the hint. I'm going to gas her, drag her and head on home. See you guys tomorrow."

262

Scenes In The Rearview Mirror

Date: **August 20, 2001**
Time: **5:45 pm**
Holiday/Event: ---
Occurrence: **The Adventures of Pierre**

It was another slow evening, and most of our customers were walking from place to place since the weather was so nice. I told my *dip*spatcher that I was stepping out for an ice cream, as I did just about every night in the summer. I went to Dairy Ann's Ice Cream Parlor, which is located next to Smudgies Pizza on North Main in Cortland. I ran into an acquaintance there, and through our conversation, I told him that I was looking for a new apartment. There was a gentleman, with salt and pepper hair, named Pierre standing behind us. Apparently, he couldn't help overhearing our conversation.

"You're looking for an apartment?" he inquired.

"Yes, I am," I replied.

"I own about forty units in Cortland, if you would like to take a look at some," he offered.

"Sure, why not. Business is slow and I have the time," I replied.

"OK, let me get my ice cream cone and I'll show you some apartments I have available," Pierre said.

John "the Milkman" Wallin

"That's cool; I have to get some ice cream too."

Soon after we had paid for our ice creams, we jumped into his truck and headed towards one of his apartment houses. As we traveled along, Pierre's cell phone rang.

"Hello, can I help you?" Pierre politely and professionally asked.

In New York, they had passed a hands-free law requiring any cell phones in use on the road to be hands free, and Pierre's phone was set up so that the caller's voice emanated from the sound system in his truck. Therefore, I could hear a woman reply, "Yes, I'm looking for a two bedroom apartment on the outskirts of the city."

Pierre thought for a few seconds and said, "We have a two bedroom apartment over by the Kmart shopping center on Route 13, if that would interest you."

"When can I see it?" the woman asked.

"I need to ask you a few questions first," Pierre countered.

"Go ahead," the woman unabashedly replied. "I have nothing to hide."

"Do you own any pets?"

"Yes, I do. Do you accept dogs?"

"It all depends on how big the dog is and how friendly it is."

264

Scenes In The Rearview Mirror

"Well, the dog is extremely friendly."

"That's cool," Pierre continued. "How big is it?"

"Well," she hedged, "what do you consider big?"

"Is it the size of a rottweiler, black lab, bichon, or chihuahua?"

"Well, it's not as big as a rottweiler. It's in between the size of a beagle and a great dane."

Pierre's brow furrowed in suspicion. "How friendly is the dog?"

"Well, it bit the postman the other day, but he was antagonizing the dog," she quickly finished.

"I can sense that this probably wouldn't work out. Thanks for calling, though," Pierre quickly replied as he hung up. The cell phone rang about two seconds later, but Pierre decided not to answer it.

"Are you usually this busy?" I inquired.

"This is our busiest time of the year since all of the college students are coming back for the fall term," he replied. "Let's go check out some apartments."

Soon after we arrived at a ten-unit apartment building on Argyle Street and Pierre showed me one of the nicer apartments.

"Here's one you may like," Pierre offered as we approached the second floor in the building. "It has one bedroom, a kitchen and, of course, a bathroom."

John "the Milkman" Wallin

"Is there a den?" I asked as we entered the apartment. "I'm writing a book and I need an area where I can put a desk, a computer and some file cabinets."

"Let me show you the closet in the hallway. It's real big and you can put everything in there, including your manuscripts."

I took a gander, but wasn't quite impressed. "Well, this is fairly large, but it's not quite what I'm looking for," I said. "Besides, there's no light in here."

"That's no problem," Pierre insisted. "I can rig something up."

"Nah. That's all right. Can you show me another apartment?"

"Sure. It's on the other side of town, though." Pierre was handling my rejection with true professionalism. "Do you have time?"

"Sure, it's not busy," I replied. "What the heck."

"Before I show you another apartment on River Street, I want you to see something at another place that I own."

We hopped back into his truck and drove to one of his apartment buildings on Elm Street. When we arrived, I took a look at the building, looked back at Pierre and said, "Are you sure this isn't a nightmare on Elm Street?" The building needed a paint job and a new roof.

Scenes In The Rearview Mirror

"It's not that bad," Pierre hedged. "Looks can be deceiving."

We jumped out of the truck and Pierre took me to the third floor where some dude lived. "Wait until you see this," Pierre chuckled.

When we got to the third floor, there was an odor that I simply couldn't describe. "Yeech! What is that disgusting odor?"

"I don't know. I've never been able to figure it out," Pierre replied as he knocked on the door. "Hey Jeremy! Open up! I have my assistant with me and I want to introduce him to you."

After a few moments, Pierre produced a key ring with a couple dozen keys on it. He selected one on the ring and unlocked the door. "Hey Jeremy," Pierre continued to call, "where are you?"

As we proceeded through the living room, I must have tripped a hundred times. "What a freaking mess!" I complained. "How does he maneuver through all of this?" There were beer bottles and pizza boxes all over the place. I somehow managed to find a chair underneath all the dirty laundry while Pierre ventured down the hallway to see if Jeremy was in his room.

"Wake up, Jeremy!" Pierre yelled.

"Arggh-mmm-cachaac," Jeremy uttered.

John "the Milkman" Wallin

"Come on, Jeremy! It's 6:30 pm and you should have been out of bed hours ago," Pierre commanded. "Get your act together!" There was a slight pause. "Gross! Put some clothes on, will ya? And come out to the living room. I want to introduce you to my assistant."

After ten minutes of waiting, Jeremy finally came out of his bedroom. He was fully clothed, but his hair was sticking up about six inches in the air. His eyes were still squinting. One of his eyes was black and he had a cut on the bridge of his nose.

"You look like hell!" Pierre exclaimed. "What happened?"

"Well, I kind of had a rough night," Jeremy answered. "I went to McDanielson's for a few beers, and when I got home, I couldn't find the lights and I tripped the dark."

"A few beers? You mean a few six-packs, don't you?" Pierre prodded.

"Whatever," Jeremy discouragingly answered.

"Splash some water in your face and try to wake up so you can play a tune on the piano for me and my assistant here."

Jeremy meandered to the kitchen sink and splashed some water on his face. He attempted to fix his hair, but gave up and came back into the living room where he sat down at the piano. As Pierre and I sat there,

Scenes In The Rearview Mirror

he began playing a piece that sounded like it might have been written by Mozart or Beethoven. After he finished, Pierre and I applauded.

"That was awesome!" I exclaimed. "Who's that by?"

"I wrote it," Jeremy replied.

I was shocked. "You're kidding! That's great!" Pierre gave me an I-told-you-so look. "Can you play another one?"

"Maybe next time, John," Pierre directed. "Thanks, Jeremy. Don't forget the two month's rent you owe me."

"You know, Jeremy," I started to say as we headed for the door, "I'm not trying to pry or anything, but you ought to try to get your act together and make something out of yourself. You have a gift, and I think you can go places. I'll see you later."

We then made our way, my new boss and I, down to the first floor and out of the building.

"Where to now, Kemosabe?" I asked, as we hopped into his truck

"I have a couple more apartments to show you on River Street, and then I have to get some dinner."

We checked out a couple more apartments on the outskirts of the city, and then Pierre drove me back to my taxi-cab at Dairy Ann's Ice Cream Parlor.

269

John "the Milkman" Wallin

"Let me know if you want any of the apartments I showed you, John, or if there are any more you'd like to see."

"Thanks, Pierre. I really appreciate it."

"No problem," Pierre said with a grin. "Just put me in your book."

I laughed. "No problem! This is just too funny to pass up!"

I hopped into my cab and radioed to Dave, "This is car fifteen; I'm back in."

"Another one of your rendezvous?"

"No, I ran into this landlord at Dairy Ann's, and he took me to see some of the apartments he has for rent."

"Yeah, yeah, this is just another of your... CUUZZZSH, the radio sounded as I stopped Dave from talking by holding the microphone button in. "Oh yeah, I also learned a very valuable lesson," I interjected as I released the button.

"What's that?" Dave returned.

"Everyone has something to offer in this life, no matter who it is."

"Well, all right, John. I'm not going to send you home this time, since your rendezvous was an important lesson."

"Thanks, Dave. Can I offer you a cup of coffee?"

270

Scenes In The Rearview Mirror

"Sure, John, why not? Are you buying?"

"No, I just wanted to know if you wanted some coffee!"

"Cheap bastard." Dave mumbled under his breath.

John "the Milkman" Wallin

Scenes In The Rearview Mirror

Date: July 4, 2002
Time: 6:00 pm
Holiday/Event: Fourth of July
Occurrence: Taxi Dream

The fourth of July had finally arrived and my boss, Uncle Sam, recruited me to work with Dave, my fellow cabbie and partner in crime.

To show my disapproval, I decided to be an hour late. When I arrived at the office at six o'clock, all the day drivers had already left, and Dave was already on the road.

"I'm in, Dave," I radioed.

"How come you're late?" Dave blasted.

"I thought I'd send a message to Uncle Sam for making me work on the Fourth of July."

"OK, I'll make sure he gets the message when I see him tomorrow."

"That's awesome," I sarcastically replied. "I'm going to step out for a cup of java now, Dave."

"Make it fast!" Dave commanded. "And none of your hour deals. Ya hear?!"

"Why not? I replied like a little kid. "There isn't any business out here."

"Just make it quick."

273

John "the Milkman" Wallin

After I got my cup of coffee, I parked behind the VFW under a tree. I figured Dave was at one of his own shady spots as well. I decided to turn my radio down, since there still wasn't any business.

A few moments later, my eyelids started drooping as they began to get heavier and heavier…

…"Where the hell am I? I feel like I'm in a jungle. And the stench around here; I feel as though I'm in hot pursuit of a wild boar! Puwee! Hey, you idiot; watch where you're going!

The drivers around here are crazy!"

"Car fifteen; John, where are you?.. Car fifteen; come in."

"I'm not sure Dave, but I'm surrounded by a bunch of huge skyscrapers, hundreds of cars and a crowd of wall to wall people. I'm also stuck in a traffic jam!"

"You'd better lay off those drugs, John! Now go get the Times Square Hotel! There's a gentleman waiting for your services."

"Where is the Times Square Hotel?"

"Same place it was when you picked up someone there last week. Quit messing around and go get the call!"

"I'm after it…Excuse me Miss, can you tell me where the Time Square Hotel is?"

"It's straight down that way, about ten city blocks."…

274

Scenes In The Rearview Mirror

…"There it is. Man, it took me long enough to get here…Hop in Mister!"

"Thanks, cabbie."

"Where are you going?"

"To Radio City Music Hall, and step on it!"

"Yes sir! Are you going to work?"

"Yeah, sort of; if you want to call what I do, work. Don't you know who I am?"

"No, I can't say that I do."

"What do you do besides drive a taxi-cab, cabbie?"

"I'm a writer, and I'm writing a book on my crazy taxi adventures."

"Cool. How long have you been working on it?"

"Oh, about two years now."

"That's great!.. You can drop me off over there. How much is it?"

"Fifteen bucks."

"Here you go."

"Hey Mister!" Don't you want your change?.. I guess I'm going to have go in after him. I hope I'll be able to get through the doorman…Excuse me doorman, I was wondering if you could let me in for a few minutes? The gentleman I just dropped off forgot his change."

"Yeah, go ahead cabbie, but make it fast."…

275

John "the Milkman" Wallin

"Thanks man…Excuse me, I was wondering if you could tell me where the tall gentleman that I just dropped off is."

"He's over there by the water cooler."

"Thanks!.. Hey Mister, you forgot your change!"

"Oh don't worry about it, cabbie."

"Thanks. I appreciate it, man. Hey, what's your name?"

"Gus; Gus Baker."

"Nice to meet you, Gus."

"What's *your* name?"

"John "the Milkman" Wallin."

"Nice to meet you as well. How would you like to be a guest on my show tonight? I'll interview you about your book."

"You're kidding me?!"

"Nope. One of our guests came down with the flu, and she can't make it."

"That would be awesome! Let me go out to my cab and tell my dispatcher that I'll be steppin' out for a while."

"No problem, take your time."…

… "Excuse me, Mr. Doorman…Hey, Dave."

"Yeah, what do you want now, fifteen?"

"Gus Baker is going to interview me on his show tonight."

276

Scenes In The Rearview Mirror

"You keep on smoking that wacky weed, and you'll wind up in Kansas being interviewed by the Wizard of Oz!"

"Yeah, whatever. I'll see you in a bit."

"Just make it fast, ya hear? And not for an hour either, whatever you're doing!"

"Boy, what a grouch. Now I'm going to have to get through that doorman again."…

"What do you want now, cabbie?"

"Gus Baker is going to interview me for tonight's show. Can you let me back in?"

"Well let me go check. I'll be right back."…

"Man, they really have tight security around here."…

… "OK, cabbie, go on in."

"Thanks, doorman. Here's a dollar. Don't spend it all in one place."

"You're a real wise guy, you know that?!"

"Yeah, yeah, whatever."…

…"Right through here Mr. Wallin. We have to prep you."

"Thanks. This place is awesome! What's your name?"

277

John "the Milkman" Wallin

"Liz."

"How long will it be until Mr. Baker interviews me, Liz?"

"You'll be going on in fifteen minutes."

"Wow, I'm starting get nervous."

"Don't worry, as soon as they start rolling the cameras, you'll be over your stage fright. You'll be just fine."

"Thanks. I feel better already."

"I'll be right back, Mr. Wallin."

"OK, I'll be waiting."…

"OK, Mr. Wallin, you're set to go on in five minutes. Walk this way."

"Thanks, Liz."…

…"The Gus Baker show will return right after these messages."…

…"Two minutes, Mr. Wallin."

"Thanks, cameraman."…

…"One minute. Get ready."…

"OK, John; go on over and have a seat. Mr. Baker will be introducing you in thirty seconds."

"Thanks, Liz."…

…"Five, four, three, two, one."

Scenes In The Rearview Mirror

"Welcome back, everyone. My next guest is a gentleman who drives a taxi-cab, and is currently writing a book on his eventful experiences. Please give him a big welcome, John "the Milkman" Wallin."

"Thank you, thank you."

"Welcome John, nice to see you."

"Thanks Gus, it's a pleasure to meet you. Thanks for the opportunity."

"My pleasure. Now, how long have been driving a cab?"

"Oh, about five years now."

"And how long have you been working on the book?"

"For two years."

"Really? How long do you think it will be before you're finished?"

"It's hard to tell. This is my first book. Maybe a few years."

"What made you decide to start such a big project anyway?"

"I've been thinking about it for quite some time now. A lot of my friends and customers have encouraged me to get into it. A few years ago I picked up a friend of mine, and after he rode around with me for a couple of hours, he saw some of the crazy things that happened to me. He

John "the Milkman" Wallin

exclaimed, 'you can't make this stuff up!' The first chapter of the book is called 'You Can't Make This Stuff Up.'"

"What are some of the other chapters about?"

"Well, the 'Police Log' chapter is about all of the crazy situations that I got into involving the police. That's one of my favorite chapters. It's very dramatic and sometimes funny as well."

"Can you tell us about some of those events?"

"Well, let me see here…"

"I'll tell you what, John, collect your thoughts, and you can share your stories with us after these messages. We'll be right back."…

…"Thirty seconds, Mr. Baker…ten seconds… five, four three two, one."

"Welcome back. We're talking with John 'the Milkman' Wallin. He's in the middle of writing his first book about the life of a taxi-cab driver. Welcome back, John."

"Thanks, Gus."

"So tell us about your experiences when you got involved with the police."

"From having a most wanted criminal sitting in the front seat of my cab, to a drug dealer who tried to get in my cab with a .30-30 Winchester he stole after a gone-wrong drug deal, I've seen it all."

Scenes In The Rearview Mirror

"That's pretty interesting. I'm afraid we're going to have to rap things up now, Mr. Milkman. We'll be right back with John "the Milkman" and his new book, right after these messages…Hey, Liz, go get our next guest ready to go on in five minutes."…

…"Ten seconds, Mr. Baker…five, four, three, two, one. You're on!"

"Welcome back ladies and gentleman. We're talking with John 'the 'Milkman' Wallin. So, do you have a guesstimate on when you think the book will hit the stores?"

"I would have to say two to three years."

"That long?"

"Yeah, well you know, these things take time, and I want it to seem like I'm on my second book, not my first. I'm going to make sure everything is perfect, even if I have to go over it a thousand times."

"Interesting. Good luck with everything."

"Thanks, Gus."

"**Scenes in the Rearview Mirror (A Cabbie's Journal)** Give it up, everybody, for John 'the Milkman' Wallin. We'll be right back with our next guest, right after this."…

John "the Milkman" Wallin

…"Car fifteen: CAR FIFTEEN! WAKE UP!" Dave abruptly interjected.

"Uhum…mmm…Where the hell am I?" I slurred.

"If you don't know that, John, you're in big trouble."

"I must be in back of the VFW, from the looks of it."

"I'm really starting to worry about you, John."

"Thanks. I'm going to step out and get a cup of coffee, Dave."

"No, you're going to get Big Joe at his trailer behind the Diner in Homer."

"Yeah ,OK Dave… Let me see; I think I'll stop real quick at Kwik Fill and get a cup of coffee on the way to get Joe. Dave will never know it. I don't want to tick him off any more than I already have.'

Just then my friend and fellow cabbie, Billy G., pulled alongside of me where I was still standing. We always would meet behind the VFW to discuss the night's events.

"Hey, John," Billy yelled, excited to see me. "How are ya?"

"Pretty good, except I don't relish the fact that I have to work on the fourth of July."

"The boss made you work?"

Scenes In The Rearview Mirror

"Yeah, Uncle Sam made me work." Billy 'the Grin' Grinnell just grinned without his usual chuckle. "What have you been doing all day, Billy?"

"I just came from a BBQ at my sister's house."

"Must be nice."

"Yeah, too bad you couldn't have been there," Billy, this time, chuckled.

"Very funny."

"Car fifteen," Dave busted in. "Car Fifteen!"

"Yeah, Dave; what do you want now?"

"Did you get 'Big Joe'?"

"No, not yet."

"What the hell have you been doing for the past umpteen minutes?"

"I had to stop at a gas station and get some gas?" I replied.

"Yeah, right. Hurry up, will ya?" Dave responded, with an aggravated tone in his voice.

"All right, all right!" I was starting to get pretty annoyed myself.

"If you weren't always drifting off into la-la land, you wouldn't have to worry about picking up your calls on time!" Dave pointed out.

"You should talk, you hypocrite!.. I have to go now, Billy."

283

John "the Milkman" Wallin

"Sounds like things are getting hot and heavy," Billy chuckled. "I think I'd better get out of here too, before the whole city explodes."

"See you later, John."

"See ya, Billy G. Have a nice day."

"You too," Billy replied.

"I don't think that's going to happen at this point," I concluded.

Billy grinned and took off, and I took off to pick up Big Joe. And we all lived happily ever after--except for Dave, of course.

King Harley's Roundtable

The month of August was drawing to a close, and a new school year was about to begin at Cortland State University.

I was becoming very unhappy with driving a cab and was seriously thinking of making a career change. I was also unhappy with the company that I was employed with, for five years, due to the company politics and internal problems.

A gentleman and friend by the name of Harley, who owned his own cab company, knew that I was about ready to quit, and offered me a position at Harley's Express Taxi.

At first things were going very well at Harley's Express. All the drivers communicated with one another and got along very well. Everyone was a team member, and the company was run like a well-oiled machine.

John "the Milkman" Wallin

I had a change of heart, and with a fresh new attitude was thinking of staying with the business until things went sour that first Saturday night.

Scenes In The Rearview Mirror

Date: **August 20, 2002**

Time: **2:23 am**

Holiday/Event: ---

Occurrence: **.30-.30 Winchester –**
20/20 Hindsight

It was a rather slow Saturday night, as the students were busy unpacking and getting ready for their first day of classes. Many of the town folks were away on vacation, and the city of Cortland looked like a ghost town.

There were just two of us working. I was cruising down the streets, and Harley was taking it easy at home, waiting to see if business was going to pick up after the bars closed. Since the office was conveniently located in his home, he was answering the phone and dispatching the calls to me as they came in.

"Hey John, you haven't fallen asleep on me, have you?" Harley radioed, in his usual short but sweet delivery.

"No Harley, I wouldn't even think of falling asleep on you! I chuckled. "What's Up?"

"That's good," Harley answered in his quick-witted dry sense of humor. His humor was usually jam-packed with only a few words. "Go get 341 North Homer Avenue."

"I'm after it," I returned. "Where are they going?"

287

John "the Milkman" Wallin

"The guy said something about Binghamton, but he's not one hundred percent sure."

"Okey Dokey."

"Just make sure, if you *do* go to Binghamton, to get the money up front."

"How much is it?"

"Fifty bucks."

Five minutes later, I pulled up in front of 341 North Homer Avenue and honked the horn. Almost immediately a tall, slim built, young man emerged from the front door. At first he seemed pretty normal, but after a few steps down the walkway he started to stumble a bit, but he recovered very quickly. He seemed to be a little under the influence of something, but mainly in control.

"Hop in," I shouted through the opened passenger side window. "Where are you going?"

"How much is it to Binghamton?" he asked as he climbed into the back seat of the passenger side.

"Fifty bucks. I'm going to need it up front though. It's just company policy."

"Take me downtown first. I have to check something out," he ordered, after several seconds of silent contemplating.

"Where are you going when we arrive downtown?"

"Just drive," he mumbled in an unsteady voice.

Scenes In The Rearview Mirror

Every time I looked into the rearview mirror, I could see the guy's eyes drifting over towards me to see what I was up to. I started to get this gut feeling that I shouldn't have picked the dude up. I was trying to figure out what he was up to.

"Where exactly are you going downtown?" I reiterated. After a moment of silence, I asked him again. "So, where exactly are you going?"

"Downtown, I told you!" he impatiently answered.

"Downtown is a very large place. Do you know exactly where you are going?" I started to become a bit impatient myself.

"I'll let you know when we get there! Just keep driving!"

As the guy was constantly looking over at me, I started to get a bit nervous. Through all of my experiences and gut instinct, I could usually figure out what someone was up to. I just didn't have a clue as to what was going on with this dude.

Even though it was only a five minute trip from where I picked the guy up to downtown, it seemed like it took forever.

"OK, here we are…beautiful downtown Cortland, New York," I continued, sounding like a tour guide in Hollywood. I thought maybe if I joked a bit it would ease the tension, but it just seemed to aggravate things further.

John "the Milkman" Wallin

I was beginning to think that the way this guy was acting, he had just done something very bad, or was about to.

"OK, on your left is one of the most popular college bars in Cortland, and on your right is the local community restaurant." I continued to joke, again, thinking that it would ease the tension – at least for me. "Would you like to get off at any of these places?" Instead of answering, his eyes that were filled with fear and anger shifted towards me once again.

"Up here on your right is Jack Danielson's Bar and on your left is Mandolin Winds," I continued. "Do any of these strike your fancy?"

"Go to the end of the road, down there further. There's a Shell gas station down there. I am going to my friend's apartment." He didn't seem like he really knew where he was.

"The only Shell gas station in town is at the end of Port Watson on the outskirts of the city."

"Go there then."

"Now we're getting somewhere," I mumbled to myself.

When we finally arrived at his destination, the suspicious dude told me to wait for him for five minutes. As he went up to his friend's apartment, two young males came over to my cab from the house next door and asked me if I could take them home.

290

Scenes In The Rearview Mirror

"Sure, hop in," I directed. "Where are you guys going?" I felt a little more at ease at that point.

"We're going to the Village Terrace Apartments on the other side of town."

"Sure, no problem," I replied. "I just have to wait for this guy who should be coming out momentarily."

"No problem," the less aggressive one responded.

"Actually, I'm thinking of taking off right now. This guy has been acting really strange, and I can't figure out what he's up to."

"That's all right, if he tries something, we'll cover your back," the more aggressive of the two responded.

"I'm going to give him one more minute." Then we'll take off."

Thirty seconds later, the guy came running down the stairs with what looked to be a shotgun in his arm.

"Holy shit!" the more aggressive guy in the back yelled. "That guy has a thirty-thirty Winchester!"

The mysterious dude rounded the front end of my car to get in on the opposite side from where the two other guys were sitting. It seemed like everything was going in slow motion.

"Damn! I yelled. "The freakin' shift is stuck! I can't get the car to go into drive!" I thought I was going to piss my pants.

291

The three seconds that had elapsed felt like three hours. As the guy with the shotgun started to open the car door, he noticed that the guy that he had stolen the gun from was coming down the stairs, out of the building. The dude, at the last split second, decided to take off on foot. I was finally able to get the car in drive and pulled a u-turn to head back towards the city.

"Duck, you guys! Let's get the hell out of here!" I yelled as my speedometer approached sixty mph. "Are you guys all right?!"

"Yeah, we're fine. Can you believe that guy?!" the less aggressive of the two yelled.

"I'm going to head towards the diner down the road and call the cops," I told the two.

When I got there, there were a few people hanging out in front and I yelled to them to go inside the diner and call the cops.

"What's going on?" one of the women asked.

"There's a guy out here running around with a shotgun!" I yelled. "Just go in there and call the cops!" I didn't want to leave my cab.

The owner of the diner came out and told everyone to get back into the diner. He then locked the front door. A few minutes elapsed and five police cars showed up. It seemed like the whole police force was there.

Scenes In The Rearview Mirror

The first officer I spoke to asked me what direction the guy was heading in. He and the other three police cars took off in the direction I told them to at lightning speed. The remaining officer started asking me a bunch of questions. After he finished questioning me, he told me that he would be in touch.

About an hour later, while I was cruising down the streets, the police had caught the guy and called me down to the police station to identify him.

John "the Milkman" Wallin

Scenes In The Rearview Mirror

Date: August 20, 2002
Time: 5:05 am
Holiday/Event: ---
Occurrence: My Fair Share and My Last Fare

After being down at the police station for an hour or so I cleaned and gassed my cab and headed to the office. When I arrived, Harley and the day crew were sitting at a table on the back porch discussing their usual daily business.

"How ya doing, guys?"

"Pretty good, John. How are you? Sid asked.

"I was shaken up a bit, but I'm all right now. I think that it's just about the worst thing that has happened to me since I started driving a cab."

"Oh, that's nothing," Sid boasted. "I picked up this dude one time who tried to rob me at gunpoint."

"No kidding?! What did you do?"

"After he pulled the trigger the second time, I grabbed the gun from the dude and I cold-cocked him with it. Then I emptied out the bullets that were in the remaining chambers."

"Do you think that he knew that the first two chambers were empty?"

295

John "the Milkman" Wallin

"Yeah. He was just a kid. He was probably just trying to scare me."

"Did he take off after you hit him?"

"No, he was out cold. I brought him to the police station and they arrested him," Sid concluded as though it was all in a day's work. "No big deal."

"Wow, that's pretty crazy. How about you, Jamey?" I asked one of the other drivers. "What is the wildest thing that has ever happened to you?"

"Well," Jamey paused, "I've had a lot of interesting things happen to me over the past ten years that I've been driving a cab, but the one thing that sticks out in my mind is when I once drove this guy, who was from Texas, to the Sheridan Hotel in Ithaca where he was staying. When I picked him up, I was going to ask him for the thirty dollars up front, but he was dressed in some really expensive clothes, and he seemed like he was very well off. I didn't want to insult him."

"You really can't tell though all the time," I interjected. "I once had a guy from New York City in my cab who'd been dressed to the hilt. When I asked him for the fare he was totally out of funds."

"Well, as it turned out," Jamey continued, "when we arrived at the Sheridan Hotel, I asked him for the thirty dollars, and he couldn't come up with it. He told me that he must have left his money in his hotel room, and that

296

Scenes In The Rearview Mirror

he was going to go in and get it. I thought for a second that I didn't want to take a chance of him not coming back out, so I told him to leave his wallet, or something of value with me until he came back. He told me that his snake-skinned cowboy boots were worth over three hundred dollars. I told him that they would do, and to try to hurry. Fifteen minutes went by, and the dude hadn't come back out."

"I would have taken off with the boots," Harley pointed out after taking a sip from his coffee.

"I thought of that at first, but I really needed the cash. I called the police on my cell phone. Coincidently, when the cops got there, the guy from Texas came back out of the hotel and told the police, and me, that he couldn't find his money. He said that he misplaced five hundred dollars and he couldn't remember where he put it. After a few minutes, while the police were trying to decide what to do, the dude remembered where he put the money."

"Where did he put it?" Sid asked.

"It was in the toe of one of his boots," Jamey replied.

"I told you, you should have taken off with his boots!" Harley exclaimed.

"Yeah, I was kind of kicking myself for not taking off," Jamey concluded. "But as it turned out the guy paid me the thirty dollars and tipped me another thirty, to boot. I thought the money that I did get was well earned."

John "the Milkman" Wallin

"How about you Harley?" Jamey passed the plate. "You've been driving a cab for twenty years or so now. You must have some pretty wild stories of your own to offer."

"Well, I don't know," Harley modestly replied.

"Come on, Harley," I pressured.

"Well…I can remember one evening about fifteen years ago. I was dispatched to pick up a pregnant woman who lived approximately eight miles out of the city. It was the third time in five days that she'd had false labor pains and called us to bring her to the hospital in Cortland. Her due date was approximately a month away."

"Yeah, sure," Sid interrupted. "Now you're going to tell us that you delivered the baby yourself."

"Almost, but not quite," Harley continued. "After we took off for the hospital, about two miles down the road, we had a flat. At that point the woman was in definite pain and I was getting really nervous. I then radioed my dispatcher and told him to call an ambulance. I mumbled to myself, 'Oh Lord, please don't do this to me.'"

"I would have been freaking out by then," I remarked.

"As the woman started breathing heavier and yelling louder, I asked my dispatcher if he had called the ambulance, and he said they were on their way. I told the woman, who was lying on her back in the back of my cab,

298

Scenes In The Rearview Mirror

to relax. I put my jacket under her head and I tried to keep her as calm as I could. As it turned out, the attendants had to deliver the baby in the ambulance."

"She was that close?" Jamey asked.

"Yeah," Harley replied. "And if I knew she was that close, I probably would have had a heart attack."

"Nah, you would have done just fine," I reassured.

"Well fellas, I'll see you around town sometime. I've had my fair share and my last fare."

"Yeah, you'll be back," Sid responded. "Once you get this taxi stuff in your blood, you can't get away from it."

"We'll see. Time will tell," I replied. "I've been thinking of leaving the business for quite some time now anyway."

"What are you going to do?" Harley asked.

"I'll probably go back into sales, or maybe radio, or both. I'll see ya."

So I hopped into my personal car and took off. When I looked into the rearview mirror, the mirror was gone. I remembered that it had broken off the day before. I shrugged my shoulders and decided that it didn't matter anyway since I was looking towards a new horizon where the brilliant morning sun was beginning to rise.

John "the Milkman" Wallin

Aforeword

I hope you enjoyed my anecdotes.

My second book "Scenes in the Rearview Mirror II (A Cabbies Convention)" is already in the works. It's a collection of anecdotes from other cabbies from all over the country, some of which blow mine away.

On the horizon will be my third book, "The B Side of the Disc (My Radio Daze)" which will be about my career as a college disc-jockey. Very funny and entertaining as well. If you would like to get a hold of me, my email address is wallinjohn55@yahoo.com. Tell me what you think.

www.authorjohnwallin.com